STAR WARS®

BOBA FETT™

MAZE OF DECEPTION

ELIZABETH HAND

LUCAS BOOKS

SCHOLASTIC INC.

New York   Toronto   London   Auckland   Sydney
Mexico City   New Delhi   Hong Kong   Buenos Aires

For my son, Tristan
— EH

www.starwars.com
www.starwarskids.com
www.scholastic.com

No part of this publication may be reproduced in whole or in part, or stored in a retrieval system, or transmitted in any form or by any means, electronic, mechanical, photocopying, recording, or otherwise, without written permission of the publisher. For information regarding permission, write to Scholastic Inc., Attention: Permissions Department, 557 Broadway, New York, NY 10012.

ISBN 0-439-44245-1

Cover art by Louise Bova

SCHOLASTIC and associated logos are trademarks and/or registered trademarks of Scholastic Inc.

12 11 10 9 8 7 6 5 4   5 6 7 8/0

Printed in the U.S.A.
First printing, April 2003

JF
HAN
PB

MAZE OF DECEPTION

Chosen by fate. Destined for conflict.

JEDI QUEST

PROLOGUE

The Dream is always the same. Boba Fett always thinks of it as *The* Dream, because it's the only one he ever remembers. The only dream he ever *wants* to remember.

In The Dream, his father, Jango Fett, is alive. He is showing Boba how to handle a blaster. The dull gray weapon is much heavier than Boba thought it would be.

"Like this," Jango says. He is not wearing his Mandalorian helmet, so Boba can see his father's brown eyes, coolly intelligent but not cold, not when he is looking at his son. When his father holds the blaster it looks weightless, a deadly extension of Jango's own hand. He hands the weapon to Boba, who tries hard to keep his hand steady as he holsters it.

"Always make certain your grip is tight," Jango goes on, "or else an enemy can knock it from you. Like this —"

1

A quick motion and the blaster falls from Boba's hand. Boba looks up in dismay, expecting a reprimand, but his father is smiling. "Remember, son — trust no one, but use everyone."

That's when Boba wakes up. Sometimes his father's message is different, and sometimes the weapon is different. A dartshooter, say, or a missile. But one thing never changes.

Boba always wakes from The Dream. And his father is still dead.

CHAPTER ONE

"Boba! Downtime's over! I need you — we're in final approach."

Boba looked up groggily from where he'd been asleep in *Slave I*'s cockpit. Beside him, where once his father would have sat at the starship's controls, the bounty hunter Aurra Sing was hunched over the console. She was staring at the screen. It was filled with symbols that were meaningless to Boba Fett — the coordinates of their precise destination remained scrambled.

"Yes!" Aurra Sing murmured triumphantly. "We're almost there."

She looked aside at Boba. Quickly he turned away. He wasn't supposed to know where they were going.

That was part of the deal. Aurra Sing would bring the two of them here, following the coordinates she had discovered in *Slave I*'s databank. The coordinates were part of a complex system — a treasure map, really — that detailed where Boba's father had stored a vast fortune in credits and precious metals, all across the galaxy.

Jango Fett had been a bounty hunter — an extremely *successful* bounty hunter. He had been an extremely clever one, too. Trained as a great Mandalorian warrior, Jango had learned the most important lesson of all: *Prepare for the worst.* And so he had made certain that his young son, Boba, would have access to his fortune after his death. The fortune could never be obtained by anyone else, because the access code was programmed so that only Boba's retinal scan and DNA could obtain it. Since Boba was the sole *unaltered* clone of his father, he and he alone shared Jango's pure genetic material.

But Boba did not know where the fortune was. Only Aurra Sing knew that, because she had accessed the records on his father's ship. The ship that should have been Boba Fett's now.

Boba looked warily at the person next to him. Her topknot of flaming red hair brilliant against dead-white skin. Her eyes blazing as twin suns.

"She is one of the deadliest fighters I have ever known," Jango had told Boba once, years before. "She was trained as a Jedi, but for some reason she hates them more than she hates anyone in the galaxy — and that's saying something! Don't ever cross her, son. And above all, don't *ever* trust her."

Boba Fett certainly didn't trust her. Who would? Aurra Sing was as thin and muscular and fine-boned as a Kuat aristocrat, but as deadly as a Mentellian savrip. She was a solitary hunter and a lethal predator.

Like my father. Like I could be, Boba thought. His glance turned admiring — though he was too smart to let Aurra Sing see *that*!

"Get ready for descent," she snapped as she punched in the final landing codes. "Soon you'll start making yourself useful to me, kid!"

The coordinates were still scrambled. But earlier, while Aurra Sing was momentarily distracted, Boba had peeked at the screen and stolen a glimpse of the itinerary data. They were somewhere in the Core Worlds. A long way from Bespin and Cloud City, where he'd met up with Aurra. Boba knew about the Core Worlds from overhearing his father's conversations. It was a good place to buy weapons — a good place to buy *anything*, now that he thought about it. Maybe a good place to outfit *Slave I* — once he got rid of Aurra Sing.

He didn't know the name of their actual destination, and he couldn't read the planet's coordinates, but he could see it on the monitor. A medium-sized planet, as gleaming and faceted as a green-and-gold jewel. He glanced at Aurra Sing, but she was busy with the landing program. He looked back at the planet on the screen. A string of unintelligible numbers and letters scrolled across it, and then a single phrase that he could understand.

AARGAU. LANDING ACCESS GRANTED.

Aargau. So that's where they were going.

Too bad I've never heard of it. Boba sighed. The landing restraints chafed his arms. When he tried to get more comfortable, Aurra Sing glared at him.

"You want to get out now?" she said, and gestured at the dumping bay. "It can be arranged!"

Boba gritted his teeth, forcing himself to smile apologetically. "Sorry."

Don't trust her, his father had said. But Boba had struck a deal with her. He had agreed — reluctantly — to split the treasure with her, fifty-fifty.

He had no choice. He had no money, no credits, no possessions except for his flight bag, his father's Mandalorian helmet, and *Slave I*. He had no friends out here, wherever *here* was. And he had no friends anywhere. Even when he had the chance of having a friend, he soon lost it.

He had only himself to rely on: an eleven-year-old with his father's training, his father's split-second reflexes, his father's fighting instincts — and his own talent for survival.

"Ready?" barked Aurra Sing. It was a command, not a question.

"Ready," said Boba, and he readied himself for their final descent to Aargau.

CHAPTER TWO

Aargau wasn't the first planet Boba Fett had ever visited, or even the second. For a kid, Boba had seen a lot of planets in a short time. There was gray, cloud-swept Kamino, his homeworld, where months could pass and you'd never see anything but sheets of silvery rain, and hear nothing but the pounding of wind and water. There was Geonosis, a vast desert planet that glowed beneath its orange rings, where Boba had buried his father; and Bogden, a small planet orbited by so many moons it looked like part of a gigantic game of Wuur-marbles.

And there was the *Candaserri*. The Republic troopship *Candaserri* wasn't a planet, of course, but it had seemed almost as big as one to Boba. On *Candaserri* he'd run into the hated Jedi, though not Mace Windu, the Jedi Knight who had killed Boba's father.

Still, except for the Jedi, *Candaserri* hadn't been so bad. It certainly wasn't as disgusting as Raxus Prime, the galaxy's toxic dumping ground, where Boba Fett had last encountered the Count. He always thought of him as "the Count," because the Count had two names — Tyranus and Dooku. Boba's father had always told his son, "If anything should happen to me, find the Count. He'll know how to help you."

As it turned out, the Count had found Boba first. The Count hired Aurra Sing to bring Jango Fett's son to him — for safekeeping, the Count assured Boba. Aurra Sing had kept *Slave I* as part of her payment, which Boba didn't think was fair — it had been his father's ship, and by rights it should be Boba's ship now.

But you didn't argue with the Count, any more than you argued with Aurra Sing.

Not if you expected to live, anyhow, Boba thought as he waited for *Slave I* to make its landing on Aargau. The Count was a tall, imperious man with icy eyes. Like Aurra Sing, he had been trained as a Jedi — although unlike Aurra Sing, the Count had finished his training and had once been a Master — which made him even more dangerous. And like Aurra Sing, the Count now hated the Jedi.

When Boba first heard his father talk about the Count, Jango referred to him as Tyranus. It was Tyranus who had recruited Jango Fett as the source for the great clone army created on Kamino. In appearance, every clone trooper resembled Jango Fett as an adult.

But only Boba Fett resembled his father as a real boy. Unlike the clone troopers, Boba's DNA had not been genetically enhanced. He grew at a normal rate, not at the accelerated rate that the clones did. Boba thought the clones were sort of creepy. They were cool, because they could fight better than any droid army, but they were strange, too, because they looked so much like his father.

The Count was even creepier. Especially since Boba knew the Count had two identities.

Tyranus had created the clone troopers now used by the Republic, while Dooku was on the side of the Republic's enemies: the Separatists. Two men on opposing sides — but they were both the same person!

And only Boba Fett knew that. He smiled now, thinking of it. *Knowing a secret is power,* his father had always told him. *But only if it remains* your *secret.*

"Ready," muttered Aurra Sing. Around them the

starship shuddered with the force of reentry. "And — *now!*"

Through the screen in front of them he had his first glimpse of Aargau. The planet's surface was invisible. All he could see was one single, impossibly huge pyramid, rising like an enormous shining steel spike from the mists of cloud far, far below.

"What's that?" asked Boba in awe. He had never seen an artifact that vast. "Is it — is that where people live?"

Aurra nodded. "Yes. Aargau is run by the Inter-Galactic Banking Clan. They're sticklers for organization and control. So a large part of the habitable portion of the planet is one gigantic pyramid. It's divided into seven levels. The upper level is the smallest, of course, so security can check all visitors coming and going. Then as you go down, you find administration, then the banks and vaults and treasuries. The merchant and living levels are below these."

Boba peered down. He could see lines zigzagging across the stepped levels of the pyramid. There were blinking lights, glowing canyons, and brilliantly colored tunnels everywhere across the pyramid's surface.

"Wow! It's like a big maze," he said admiringly.

"That's right. Droids are programmed to find their way around all the levels, but people can spend years memorizing the access codes and charts, and still get lost. They say that if you get off on the wrong level, you can spend your entire life wandering around and never find your way back to where you started."

Cool! thought Boba. He glanced furtively at Aurra Sing. Once he had his share of his father's fortune, maybe he could lose Aurra in this planetary labyrinth, regain control of *Slave I* — and regain his freedom, too. He felt in his pocket for the book his father had left him. It was the possession that Boba treasured above all else, except for his father's Mandalorian helmet.

The helmet was safe in Boba's sleeping area. But the book he had recently decided to keep with him always. It contained information and advice that his father had recorded for him. In a way, it was like having a link to his father, even though Jango Fett was dead.

But Boba didn't want to think about that. Once he had made certain the book was where it should be, he turned his attention back to the screen.

Slave I was approaching the top of the glittering pyramid. Far below, Boba could see flickers of light, green and red and blue. It made everything look like part of a gigantic circuit board. He pointed to where the deepest reaches of the planet sparkled brilliantly.

"What's down there?" he asked. "At the very lowest level?"

"That's the Undercity, kid. They say that anything goes down there — if you can find your way."

She leaned back in the command seat, grinning as the ship's computer finally made contact with the planet's security force. On the screen in front of her, green letters scrolled — not the scrambled coordinates, but letters that Boba could read clearly.

WELCOME TO AARGAU
YOUR ARE NOW ENTERING A
NEUTRAL ZONE

"Hah!" said Aurra Sing. She unfastened her safety harness and stood, shaking back her topknot mane of red hair. "Neutral zone! No such thing!"

"What do you mean?" asked Boba. He slid from his chair and followed her to *Slave I*'s docking bay.

"I mean nobody's ever neutral. Not really. Everyone and everything has a price — you just have to figure what it is." Reflexively she checked her weapons, then glanced at Boba. "I guess you're ready — all we need is *you*, after all. Let the bank check your identity and hand over the money!"

She grinned, then punched in the code to open the starship's outer doors. "Come on, kid — let's go get rich!"

CHAPTER THREE

Boba quickly decided that Aargau was definitely the cleanest planet he'd ever been on. The docking zone was like the inside of a gigantic holoscreen, with flashing lights and low, brightly colored buildings. The streets were broad and empty of any vehicles, except for a couple other airspeeders that had recently landed. There were few people or droids that he could see. Not even his father's spartan apartment on Kamino had been as clean as this!

And everything was bathed in red light — a harsh light that made Boba's eyes sting.

"Is the atmosphere this color?" he wondered.

Aurra Sing shook her head. "No. That's from special infrared rays," she explained, as they clambered out of *Slave I*. "Aargau has human-standard atmosphere. Every level is color-coded. It's supposed to make it easier to find your way around. It gives me a headache."

"Me, too." Boba rubbed his eyes. "So this level is red?"

"That's right. Infrared rays help disinfect incoming ships — and visitors. Aargau has a *lot* of rules."

Several uniformed soldiers walked among the other ships at the docking site. Even in uniform, with their faces hidden by their helmets, Boba recognized them. They were clone troopers, members of the clone army created by Count Tyranus. Aargau was part of the Republic, which would explain why the clones were here. In one of the other docking bays, Boba recognized a Republic gunship. That was where the clone troopers would have come from.

But why was a gunship here? Was it refueling?

Boba watched as the troopers drew nearer. It was a weird feeling, seeing the clones again. Boba knew that every one of them had his father's face. His father's eyes, his father's mouth — but not his father's smile. Because the clones rarely if ever smiled.

Boba could see Aurra Sing tensing as the troopers approached them. But they only nodded politely. They gave a cursory look at *Slave I*, then moved on.

"They didn't search us," said Boba in surprise. He glanced back at the troopers. "Or the ship."

Aurra shrugged. "Not really their job. They're

fighting battles, not checking cargo. Anyway, nobody bothers smuggling anything *into* Aargau. Too affluent. They've got a saying — 'Better poor on Aargau than wealthy anywhere else.' This is the bank for the whole galaxy. There's enough precious metals in vaults on Aargau to outfit an entire army a thousand times over."

"Really?" Boba grinned slyly to himself. If the bank here was that rich, would it even notice if a few bars of gold were missing?

As though she could read his thoughts, Aurra Sing added, "It's easy getting *onto* Aargau. Getting *off* is more difficult — you don't want to know what they do to people they catch trying to smuggle stuff off-planet." She turned and gave him a nasty grin. "Don't even *think* of double-crossing me, kid. All they have to do is suspect you of smuggling, and you're history. 'Cause who is an officer going to believe? An adult or a kid?"

Not just a kid — a bounty hunter's kid, thought Boba, and scowled. But he said nothing.

"So just you stay with me," Aurra Sing hissed as they headed toward a large, shining console desk. An immense holosign flickered in the air above it. The holosign had a scrolled message that repeated itself over and over and over again in a hundred different languages.

WELCOME TO AARGAU,
JEWEL OF THE ZUG SYSTEM!
OBSERVE THE FOLLOWING RULES:

I. NO UNLAWFUL REMOVAL OF
PRECIOUS METALS
II. NO POSSESSION OF WEAPONS
EXCEPT BY AARGAU CITIZENS
III. NO WILLFUL CONSPIRACY TO
DEFRAUD, DISCREDIT, OR DECEIVE
THE BANK OF AARGAU

THE ABOVE CRIMES ARE PUNISHABLE
BY IMMEDIATE EXECUTION

Boba glanced at Aurra Sing. She would have a little trouble with Rule Number II, he thought.

But Aurra Sing didn't bother to read the rules. She strode right through the holosign and into Customs Central. Boba hurried to catch up with her.

"Welcome to Aargau," said the attendant at the Customs Central console. She was humanoid, with the telltale gauntness and pallid skin that marked her as a member of the InterGalactic Banking Clan, from Muunilinst. She wore an expensive-looking, gold-and-silver plasteel suit. Its buttons looked like real platinum, with insets of blinking, emerald-colored gavril eyes. She held up a small retinal scanner, directing it first at Boba's eyes, then Aurra's. After the scan was complete, she glanced back down at the device's readout. Her expression betrayed nothing.

"May I ask the purpose of your visit?" she asked.

"I am this boy's guardian, appointed by his family to see that he gets the education he deserves," Aurra lied. Boba winced at the thought of being related to her. "We're here to check on the status of his High-Yield Universal Institutional Savings Account."

"Very good." The attendant smiled blandly. "And may I see proof of your investment?"

For a moment Aurra Sing said nothing. Then she slid a small shiny card across the desk toward the attendant. Boba's eyes widened: The card had to be encoded with the access information to his father's secret fortune!

Aurra Sing looked at the attendant and said, "I think you'll find everything you need there."

The attendant slipped the card into a new scanner. The scanner beeped and blinked. The attendant read the information display.

"Yes," she said. She looked over at Boba. "You are Boba Fett?"

Boba nodded and the attendant smiled. "With this kind of card, I'd guess you're quite a wealthy young man!"

"Yes," Boba agreed. But he certainly didn't feel — or look — wealthy! He glanced down at what he was wearing. Blue-gray tunic over blue-gray pants, knee-high black boots. Standard-issue stuff, not the way a rich kid would dress.

Would that make any difference to the security people here on Aargau? The security attendant certainly didn't seem to care. She glanced again at the shiny information card Aurra Sing had given her, still in its slot on her desk.

She said, "As first-time visitors to Aargau, you are cleared to visit Levels One through Three. That is where off-world banking accounts and precious metals are stored. Your own credits will be on one of those levels. Once you have withdrawn your credits or metals from your account, you may purchase clearance to Levels Four and Five. Level Four is where you can arrange for lodging, and Level Five is where you can buy supplies."

"What's on Level Six?" asked Boba.

"Entertainment and recreational facilities."

Boba grinned. "And Level Seven?"

The Customs attendant gave him a cool smile. "Level Seven is the Undercity. A young person like yourself would have no business there. We encourage free trade, of course, so we don't restrict merchants or traders from anywhere in the galaxy. As a result, you can find some very shady characters in the Undercity. It is terribly dangerous, especially with the recent skirmishes against the Separatists. The Republic has sent a peacekeeping force to make certain that its investments remain protected."

She continued to gaze at Boba, and went on. "You must also be sure not to exchange your money with anyone who is not a licensed member of the InterGalactic Banking Clan. There are black market money changers on Aargau. It is illegal to do business with them. If you're caught, you will be deported immediately. And you *will* be caught. Do you understand?"

Boba nodded seriously. "Yes," he said.

Beside him, Aurra Sing fidgeted impatiently. "Thanks," she said. She started to reach for the info card. "Now, if you don't mind —"

But before she could move, the attendant raised her hand. Seemingly out of nowhere, several

S-EP 1 security droids appeared and swarmed toward the desk. They were followed by a third droid that made Boba's heart pound in fear and amazement —

An IG assassin droid.

CHAPTER FOUR

Boba heard Aurra suck her breath in sharply. Behind the desk, the attendant made a slashing motion with her hand. The assassin droid stopped. Slowly it raised one arm.

Its lasers were pointed right at Aurra Sing!

Instinctively the bounty hunter went into a defensive stance. "Call it off!" she ordered the attendant.

But the attendant only shook her head. "I told you," she said in her calm voice. She was staring at Aurra's blaster."You'll have to leave your weapons here."

"Not on your life!" Aurra Sing said. She reached for her blaster. But she stopped abruptly when she saw the assassin droid reach for its concussion grenade.

"Oh," said Aurra. She withdrew her hand from her blaster. "Sorry! I guess I overlooked that detail.

I was so busy with everything else I was thinking about."

Aurra looked at Boba and smiled — a smile that was more like a grimace. "Right, Boba?"

"Yeah," said Boba. He hoped the grin he gave the attendant didn't look as fake as Aurra Sing's. "We were so excited about finally landing here, we just forgot!"

The attendant turned away from Aurra to smile indulgently at him. "I'm sure you did."

Boy, are grown-ups dumb! thought Boba. He knew that the weapons check was the only thing that could separate him from Aurra — right away.

"But you still must leave your weapons here," the attendant went on. She looked back at Aurra Sing — only this time she didn't smile. "The penalty is death. This is your last warning."

Aurra Sing scowled. "I never go anywhere un-armed."

"Didn't you read the planetary bylaws?" The attendant began to recite in a monotone. "'No unlawful removal of precious metals. No possession of weapons except by Aargau citizens —'"

Aurra cut her off quickly. "Can I leave them on my ship?"

The attendant nodded. "Very well. But you will have to be escorted by Security Personnel." She gestured to the uniformed security guards who stood watching from a few feet away. In the distance, Boba saw other uniformed figures milling about. Some had their faces hidden behind helmets; others were bareheaded.

"I need a Sigma Red escort," the attendant announced into her comlink. "She has permission to return to her ship," she said to the droids, and made another slashing gesture.

At the attendant's command, the droids retreated. At the same time, two of the uniformed security guards walked over to the desk.

"Is there trouble here?" one of them demanded. He looked suspiciously at Aurra Sing.

Boba felt his heart start to pound again.

What if they were *both* forced to leave Aargau before he got the fortune his father had left for him? He'd be as bad off as he was before. Worse, actually — because he'd be stuck with Aurra Sing!

But Aurra seemed to be thinking the same thing. Her expression suddenly grew calculating. She gave the security guard the same fake smile she had given the attendant a minute before.

"I'm cooperating, officer," she said. But the look she gave Boba was anything but glad.

The clone guard continued to watch Aurra suspiciously. The attendant looked at her, too. She pointed at Aurra Sing.

"Please escort her back to her ship," the attendant said.

The guards flanked the bounty hunter, one on either side.

"See that her weapons are properly stowed away on board," the attendant went on. She looked at Aurra. "Once you have done that, the guards will escort you back to this desk. Then I will give you your final clearance, and you can access the other levels here on Aargau."

Aurra Sing glared at the attendant. She looked at the attendant's uniform: She was wearing a blaster.

"What about you?" snapped Aurra. "You're armed!"

"Don't you listen?" the attendant asked in disbelief. "Citizens may carry arms. In fact, it is unlawful for citizens of Aargau to *not* carry weapons."

Aurra Sing turned to stare at Boba. "What about him?" she demanded. Aurra pointed at Boba angrily. "Why aren't the guards on him?"

The attendant looked at Boba. He made sure to appear as young and innocent as possible — this was the chance he'd been looking for. The attendant shook her head, almost in sympathy for the boy.

"He is not armed," she said in her calm voice. "On Aargau, free citizens may come and go as they please, once they have received clearance. This boy has received clearance. And he has broken no rules. He can decide for himself."

She turned to Boba. "Boba Fett. Do you want to accompany your guardian to the ship? Or do you want to remain here?"

Freedom! "I'll wait here," he said, trying not to let his excitement show.

For a moment he thought Aurra would lunge at him. But then she seemed to think better of it. After all, would a real guardian attack her charge?

"You better wait!" she snapped. "I'll be right back, so you better not move!"

The guards stood beside her, glaring. Aurra turned.

"Let's get this over with," she said. She started walking toward *Slave I,* a guard at either side.

But when they reached the docking bay she

looked back at Boba one last time. Her face was calm, but he could see the rage in her eyes.

Still, when she was out of sight, Boba couldn't help grinning to himself. At last. He was on his own.

CHAPTER FIVE

Boba stared at the shadow that was *Slave I*, waiting in the docking bay. He could no longer see Aurra or the guards.

But he liked looking at the ship — *his* ship. The Mandalorian helmet his father had left him was still on board, where Boba had stored it, safe from Aurra Sing. He wished now that he had thought to bring the helmet with him. It had saved his life when he wore it, back on Raxus Prime.

And, with the helmet on, he could be mistaken for an adult. That could be useful, sometimes.

But other times — like now — it was also useful to be a kid. No one expected a kid to be as smart as Boba was, or as self-sufficient. No one expected a kid to know that Dooku and Tyranus were the same person.

And no one expected a kid might have plans that didn't include a parent or guardian. Especially a guardian like Aurra Sing, who was only using him — and would get rid of him the moment she didn't need him anymore. He had no doubt about that.

Boba knew he only had a very short time until Aurra returned from the ship. When she got back, he would have to go with her to one of the lower levels to get his father's fortune. Boba knew she could not be trusted. If she had the chance, she would double-cross him.

And she has no right to the money at all, Boba thought angrily. *My father intended that fortune for me! Not some other bounty hunter — and especially not Aurra Sing!*

But without Aurra, he had no way of knowing where to find his father's treasure. It was somewhere here on Aargau — but where? The attendant had said it would be on one of the first three levels—but each level was enormous. Without any credits, Boba might as well be back on toxic Raxus Prime.

He sighed loudly. Then, remembering where he was, he turned a little worriedly and looked at the attendant in her boring Banking Clan uniform.

He expected her to be watching him. Isn't that what grown-ups did? Watched you all the time, so you couldn't move, or even think, on your own? Boba hated it, just as much as his father had hated any kind of supervision, by the Bounty Hunters' Guild — or anyone else.

But the attendant seemed to have forgotten all about Boba Fett. She stood behind the desk with her back to him. She was talking into a communicator and scanning a computer screen. Boba had just started to turn away again, when something shiny on the desk caught his eye.

The info card! Aurra Sing had forgotten to take it back!

It was still in its slot on the desk, gleaming softly in the harsh red light.

"Wow!" Boba whispered to himself in excitement.

If he could get it, he might be able to use it to locate his father's fortune!

Boba looked around furtively. Across the plaza, the security droids hovered near a bank of turbolift doors. On the other side of the plaza, a group of uniformed guards stood at ease, talking. Several people wearing clothes that identified them as members of the Banking Clan were walking toward the desk.

In a minute they would be here. The attendant would turn to greet them —

And Boba would lose his chance! Quickly, he reached across the desk. For an instant his hand hovered above the shining card. Then, quick as lightning, he grabbed it.

That was easy! he thought. He glanced at the desk. The attendant still had her back to him — but as he watched, she began to turn.

Quickly, Boba put his head down.

Don't run, he thought, even though every nerve in his body was firing *RUN!*

Don't look back — even though every second he imagined the attendant noticing and shouting at him to stop. He began to walk away, as fast and as silently as he could. He crossed the plaza, his head still down, his sweating hand clutching the shining card. He headed toward the turbolifts that descended to the lower levels.

Don't look back, he kept repeating to himself. *Don't look back!*

But more than anything, that was what he was dying to do — look back, and see if Aurra Sing was leaving *Slave I*.

Any minute now she would return.

He forced himself to keep going. It was one of the hardest things he'd ever done. Boba's instinct, always, was for action — to run, to fight, to outwit anyone who tried to stop him. But right now, only silence and stealth would save him.

And the ability to blend in. To *not* draw attention to himself.

Boba stared at the floor beneath him, cold and red and gleaming, clean as everything on Aargau was clean. Maybe twenty meters ahead of him was the wall, and the rows of huge turbolifts. What was it the attendant had said about them? Boba tried to remember.

As first-time visitors to Aargau, you are cleared to visit Levels One through Three. This is where off-world banking accounts and precious metals are stored. Your own credits will be on one of those levels.

Boba's hand tightened around the shining card he had snatched from the desk. If it gave him access to his father's credits, he could get it all for himself — and leave Aurra Sing out of the deal completely!

The thought made Boba hopeful. Then, suddenly, from behind him came footsteps.

"Hey," someone called. "You — !"

Boba's throat grew tight. His hope faded. He had forgotten one of the first rules of bounty hunters — stealth.

He had let himself be seen.

"You!" the voice came again — a familiar voice. "I said, wait!"

Boba's heart was hammering inside his chest. He looked straight ahead, to where the wall of turbolifts loomed. They were just a few yards off now. There were a lot of doors, but one of them should open soon. If he sprinted, he might make it — or he might be captured by whoever was behind him.

Boba didn't look back. His hand clutched the shiny card — the key to what was rightfully his. His heart was pounding so hard his chest hurt. A few steps ahead of him he could hear the grinding sound of more turbolifts moving upward. They slowed to a halt as they approached the Security Level.

"Hey — !"

The voice came again, directly behind him!

Run! thought Boba.

He sprinted the last few steps. Immediately before of him, a line of green lights blinked above another turbolift door.

"*Approaching Security Level One,*" a mechanized voice announced. "*Please stand back from the doors.*"

Boba jumped forward. In front of him, the green lights turned to red. Someone touched his shoulder. Boba stared straight ahead, his heart thumping. The turbolift doors slid open.

"*Security Level One!*" the mechanical voice repeated. "*Please let passengers out.*"

Dozens of people hurried from the turbolift. Boba darted between them, until he was inside. He was breathing hard. But he was alone in the turbolift!

"You!" shouted the same, strangely familiar voice.

Boba whirled.

"*Now leaving Security Level One,*" said the mechanical announcement.

The doors began to slide shut. There were only inches left before it closed.

Boba let his breath out. He was safe!

With a cry a small figure lunged through the gap. The turbolift doors hissed shut. Quickly, Boba shoved the shining card into his pocket. Then he backed up against the wall and faced his pursuer.

He was trapped!

CHAPTER SIX

Boba had his back to the wall. His hands tensed to fight —

But fight who? Or *what*? Boba let his breath out in shock.

Because for a moment, he thought he was staring into a mirror. He saw his own face, his own body, his own hands raised protectively. Even the clothes were the same — same gray-blue tunic, same high black boots. The only difference was that the boy staring at Boba Fett wore a helmet.

But it wasn't a clone trooper's helmet, or a Mandalorian helmet. This was a tan helmet with gold-plated metal fittings. Boba had seen thousands like it, back on his homeworld of Kamino. It was a learning helmet, part of the equipment clone youth wore to enhance their training.

Boba was staring at his clone twin!

The two of them looked warily at each other,

keeping their arms raised in a fight posture. After a minute, the clone shook his head. He held his hand out to Boba. For the first time Boba saw that he held something.

"You dropped this," the clone said. He offered it to Boba. "Up there, by the security desk."

Boba looked at it in disbelief. It was his book — the book his father had left him. Boba shook his head. Finally he took it from the other boy.

"Thanks," Boba said. He'd been so busy trying to leave before Aurra Sing returned that he'd forgotten he had the book with him. He looked at the boy and ventured a smile. To his surprise, the boy smiled back.

"I thought it might be important," the clone said. "I'm glad I caught up with you."

Around them the turbolift descended smoothly, silently. Above the door a stream of blinking lines and numerals indicated that they were slowly approaching Level Two, thousands of meters below the first level. Boba put the book back into his pocket, beside the shining card. The boy clone looked at him curiously.

"You're not wearing a helmet," the clone said. He tapped at his own helmet. "Are you an odd or even?"

"An odd or an even?" Boba repeated. "What do you mean?"

Then he remembered.

All young clones were numbered. All young clones wore learning helmets like the one worn by the boy in front of him. The only difference was that some of the learning helmets had gold-colored hardware. Others had plain black metal hardware. Odd-numbered clones wore gold. Even-numbered clones wore plain.

This boy's helmet had gold plating. He was an odd. He was still staring at Boba, patiently waiting for a reply.

"Oh," said Boba at last. "I'm, uh, same as you. Odd."

The boy clone nodded seriously. "Is your helmet getting repaired, too?" He tapped his own helmet, making a face as a burst of static came out of the earpiece. The noise was loud enough that even Boba could hear it.

"That's why I'm here," the clone went on. "I should have remained on board with the others. But my helmet has been malfunctioning. Our commander said it would be faster to just get it repaired here, down on the Tech Support Level."

"Tech Support?" said Boba.

"Level Three. That's where all repairs are done." He looked at Boba and, for the first time, frowned slightly. "You should know that. Your helmet really *must* have malfunctioned."

Boba knew that the learning helmets provided a constant stream of data that the young clones absorbed. Some of the information was spoken through the earpieces. Some of the information was visual, streaming across the small screen that protruded from the helmet to cover this boy's left eye. Clones developed at twice the speed of normal humans. They grew twice as fast, and by using the learning helmets, their brains developed twice as fast, too.

"That's right," said Boba slowly. "I was on my way down to see if it's been repaired."

The clone nodded. He smiled again, and Boba wondered if his friendliness might be a result of his malfunction. Clones were usually not very emotional.

And even though there were hundreds of thousands of them, they were always alone.

Like me, thought Boba in mild surprise. For the first time he smiled back.

"I'm 9779," said the clone. "What designation are you?"

Boba thought fast. "1313," he said.

"I'm from Generation Five Thousand," the clone went on. "Is that your Generation, too?"

"Uh, yeah," said Boba. He hoped he wouldn't have to answer any more questions. Still, he was curious himself. He asked, "Why are all the troopers here on Aargau?"

"You mean us?" 9779 looked surprised. "You better get your helmet fixed if you forgot that! There are rumors that Separatists are here on Aargau. This is a neutral planet, but we clone troopers are supposed to keep an eye on them. Just in case of trouble."

Just in case, Boba repeated to himself. He wondered why the army would've brought a clone whose training was not complete. This had to be *part* of the training — going to a relatively stable world to learn how to patrol and defend.

"We are now approaching Level Two," the turbo-lift's mechanical voice intoned. "Please stand back from the doors."

9779 obediently moved aside. Boba started to head for the door before it opened, but the clone stopped him.

"Did you forget?" 9779 asked, his face serious. "We're going to Level Three. Got to get your helmet back!"

"Oh —" Boba stammered. "I, uh —"

But then the doors began to open. And Boba didn't have to worry about *just in case of trouble*.

Because trouble had found him. Standing outside the turbolift was —

Aurra Sing!

CHAPTER SEVEN

Boba darted to one side, behind 9779. The clone stood, oblivious, as a small group of people waited to get into the turbolift with them. In the front of the little crowd stood Aurra Sing, her face dark with anger. When she saw 9779, she gave a low laugh of triumph.

"Gotcha!" she crowed, and lunged for the clone.

"Hey — !" said 9779, confused, as Aurra Sing grabbed his arm.

"Sorry," said Boba under his breath to the clone. "But this is my stop."

Other people were crowding into the turbolift now. Before Aurra Sing could spot him, Boba squeezed between the newcomers, out onto Level Two. Behind him he could hear the clone's protests getting louder.

"— let go of me! I'll have you deported!"

"I told you to wait for me!" said Aurra Sing furiously. "Did you think you'd get that money for yourself?"

That's right! said Boba to himself. He moved quickly away from the turbolift. *That's exactly what I thought!*

The mechanized voice made its final announcement. Then the sleek metal doors closed, and the turbolift descended once more.

Boba was on his own again.

Just how he liked it!

He quickly checked to make sure he still had his father's book and the data card.

He did. He smoothed his hair, wishing again that he had his Mandalorian battle helmet to help disguise his appearance. He wasn't sure if he wanted to be mistaken for a clone again — next time he might not be so lucky. He turned and began to look around.

He was in a long, shimmering green tunnel. As a matter of fact, everything around him had a greenish glow — the walls, the floor, even the people.

And there were people everywhere. Thousands of them! He saw representatives of every race he could imagine — Gotals, Twi'leks, Dugs, Ithorians, and many more — as well as beings he didn't recognize at all. Mingled among them was an occasional clone trooper. They were easy to recognize in their sleek white body armor. Even they had a green glow on Level Two.

But mostly, he saw members of the InterGalactic Banking Clan. They were tall, thin figures in distinctive drab uniforms. Their faces were dead-white, their cheeks sunken like those of San Hill, who Boba had seen on Geonosis. Boba knew they never ventured outdoors. They spent their entire lives inside, managing their vast stores of currency.

If I was rich, I wouldn't waste my life indoors, Boba thought.

No — not IF I was rich —

WHEN *I'm rich!*

He put his hand in his pocket. He touched the smooth card that would lead him to the treasure.

If only he knew how to find it!

But where to start?

Boba frowned. Then he heard the mechanized turbolift voice behind him.

Now approaching Level Two.

Uh-oh. The first thing he better do was get away before Aurra Sing discovered his deception. He looked around.

Level Two was much bigger than Level One. There was a central area — that was where Boba

44

was standing now. And, extending out from this central area, there were tunnels. Hundreds of them, shining green tunnels with moving walkways. A nonstop stream of people went in and out of the tunnels. They stepped onto the walkways, which led them away.

Where did they go?

Boba walked a safe distance from the busy turbolift area. He went toward one of the tunnel entrances. There was a sign above it.

FIRST ROYAL BANK OF M'HAELI

Boba turned and looked at the next tunnel.

BOTHAN INDEPENDENT TREASURY

"Huh," he said. He looked at another tunnel, and another.

N'ZOTH BANKS ONLY
REGISTERED BANK OF AMMUUD,
CORPORATE HEADQUARTERS

"Banks," murmured Boba to himself. "They're all banks."

That's what the tunnels were. Every tunnel led

to a bank, or treasury, that belonged to a particular planet. He turned slowly in a circle, looking at all the tunnels stretching in every direction.

There weren't just hundreds of them. The galaxy contained untold numbers of planets. Even if only some of these had representative banks on Aargau, there might be *thousands* of them!

How could he ever figure out which one held his father's treasure?

Boba fingered the card in his pocket. Around him a steady flow of people went by. No one paid him any attention. After a minute he put the card back into his pocket, and slowly took out his father's book.

It wasn't just a book, though. Boba walked over to a quiet spot a short distance from one of the tunnels. There he opened the black book.

Inside there were no pages. There was a message screen. The first time he had opened it, after his father's death, he had seen his father's face and heard his father's words.

"There are three things you need, now that I am gone," his father's image had said. "The first is self-sufficiency. For this you must find Tyranus to access the credits I've put aside for you. The second is knowledge. For knowledge you must find

Jabba. He will not give it; you must take it. The third and the most important is power. You will find it all around you, in many forms.

"And one last thing, Boba. Hold on to the book. Keep it close to you. Open it when you need it. It will guide you when you read it. It is not a story but a Way. Follow this Way and you will be a great bounty hunter someday."

Hold on to the book. Boba bit his lip in remorse and anger. How could he have left it up on Level One? If it weren't for Clone 9779 —

Boba shook his head. No time for remorse now.

But, he thought, *if I ever see that clone again, I owe him a favor. A really, really big one.*

CHAPTER EIGHT

Boba looked around. He could barely see the turbolifts from here — too many crowds. That meant Aurra Sing would have trouble spotting him, at least for a little while. He glanced from one tunnel to the next, all of them glowing silver-green in the eerie light of Level Two.

Did one of them hold the treasure?

It was like a puzzle. Or no — it was like a labyrinth. A maze. And beneath this level was another level, and then another, levels upon levels extending for kilometers to the surface of Aargau, where the Undercity was. Even if he ever claimed his credits, how could he find his way around? Would he be able to get back to Level One and his ship?

Mazes upon mazes. His father had told him once about being captured and imprisoned in an underground labyrinth on Belsavis and another time on Balmorra. A deadly scorpionlike kretch insect hunted him through the tunnels.

"How did you escape?" Boba had asked breathlessly.

"By keeping my head," his father replied. "Mazes are designed to confuse you. To disorient you. But mazes always have an inner logic. Someone had to design them, after all. If you can stay calm and think, you can always find your way out — if you have enough time."

Boba shook his head. He looked at the vast number of tunnels around him.

No one had enough time to check out every one of them!

He glanced down at the book, still in his hands. *Open it when you need it*, his father had said.

Well, I sure need it now! thought Boba. He opened it.

The message screen was gray and blank. But slowly, as he stared down at it, letters appeared.

NEVER SEEK OUT HELP, the screen read.

Boba read the message over and over. Finally he closed the book and put it back in his pocket.

Never seek out help. He looked around at the thousands of silver-green tunnels. If he didn't ask for help here, how would he ever find his way?

"Excuse me," said a small voice beside him.

Boba jumped, his hands thrust out in a fighting posture. Next to him was a little figure, not even as tall as he was. It had a vaguely donkeyish face, pale yellow in color, with large pointed ears that swooped out from either side of its head like wings. It wore plain yellow homespun pants and a vest over a matching yellow shirt. Its hands and face were covered with short, soft fur.

It was a Bimm, Boba realized. A native of Bimmisaari.

"I could not help noticing that you seem a bit confused," the Bimm went on in its singsong voice. "May I be of assistance?"

"Uh," stammered Boba. Then he remembered what his father's book had said.

Never seek out help.

Boba glanced nervously, across to where the turbolifts were discharging more passengers onto Level Two.

Could that flash of red and white, fast as crimson lightning, be Aurra Sing? Or was he just imagining it?

The Bimm said, "I am Nuri. An independent money exchanger." Nuri gestured at the teeming crowds around them. "It is confusing, is it not? Especially when one is a first-time visitor to Aargau. Might this be your first visit?"

Boba looked at Nuri suspiciously. But the Bimm's

singsong voice was friendly, his small bright eyes warm and welcoming. Besides, Boba was a whole head taller than the little alien. Reluctantly, Boba admitted, "Ye-e-es — it is my first visit."

The Bimm nodded wisely. "I thought so. Much of my business consists of helping people like yourself. Making their time here easier. Visitors from all over the galaxy come to Aargau —"

Nuri swept his little hand out. A group of brightly dressed Mrissi swarmed past them, their brilliant feathers peeking from long robes. Close behind them a group of security guards paced watchfully in formation. Behind the guards were more members of the Banking Clan.

This group, however, seemed different from the others of the Clan. Boba stared at them, frowning. There were more heavily armed guards, for one thing. And a number of security droids — lots of S-EP1s. In the middle of them all walked a very tall, very thin man with a face lean and sharp as a razor. Two lieutenants flanked his sides.

"That is San Hill," said Nuri in a low voice. "He is the head of the InterGalactic Banking Clan."

"He looks like a big stick insect," said Boba, not wanting the Bimm to know he'd seen San Hill before.

Nuri tried to hide a smile. "Perhaps. But he is one of the most powerful men in the galaxy. His presence here, now, is very interesting indeed."

The two of them turned and watched as the procession disappeared into one of the eerie green tunnels.

When they were gone, Nuri said, "But enough of that!" The Bimm put a small, furred hand upon Boba's shoulder. "Tell me, what is the nature of your business on Aargau?"

Boba started to reply. But the words stuck in his throat. From the corner of his eye he had seen another flash of red and white, darting across the far side of the crowded level.

This time, there was no doubt that it was Aurra Sing.

CHAPTER NINE

The Bimm's face creased with concern. "What is it?" he asked.

Boba said nothing. He started to move very slowly back, going into a half-crouch. Nuri turned and let his gaze flick across the crowds moving everywhere around them. After a moment he drew his breath in sharply.

"You have made an impressive enemy, young man," he said in his fluting voice. On the far side of the great space, Aurra Sing's muscular figure could be glimpsed. She was standing near the turbolifts, scanning the area with her keen eyes. Nuri glanced at Boba, then took a step back to stand beside him. "A bounty hunter! And not just any bounty hunter, but the legendary Aurra Sing!"

Boba looked down at the Bimm. He was surprised to see that the little alien did not look frightened. Instead, he looked impressed.

That made Boba feel a bit better. "Yes," he said.

"I, uh — I had some business with her. You see, I'm a bounty hunter, too. Or will be, when —"

The Bimm raised one small, furred hand. "You need say no more. *My* business is your welfare. But I suggest we discuss that elsewhere!"

Quickly, the Bimm grasped Boba's arm. "This way," Nuri said. He pointed to a small, dark passage a short distance away.

Boba glanced back over his shoulder. Aurra Sing was gone. A security droid now stood where she had been.

"Oh, no!" Boba said under his breath. He felt a stab of panic. Aurra could be anywhere, behind anyone. . . .

He had been careless. And his carelessness could cost him his fortune — or his life.

"Quickly!" whispered Nuri. "Come —"

Boba hesitated. He didn't know anything about this small, pointy-eared alien. Nuri looked harmless enough, but —

But Boba had no choice. If he remained here, he'd be playing hide-and-seek with Aurra Sing, with a bunch of clone troopers for an audience.

"Okay," said Boba. He followed Nuri toward the dark passage. "I'm coming."

Unlike the other tunnels, this one was narrow and dim. It had a low ceiling and rounded walls.

There was no blinking sign overhead to identify it. A small panel was set into one wall beside the entrance. The panel had a lot of buttons on it. Nuri pressed the buttons in a pattern Boba tried to follow. An instant later the wall slid open to reveal a second, hidden passage.

"This way," said Nuri. He ducked into the passage, with Boba at his heels.

The door closed behind them. Boba straightened, blinking. They were in a small, circular room. Instead of the eerie green light that colored everything on Level Two, the light in here was soft and yellow. Soothing, like Nuri's voice.

"Where are we?" asked Boba.

The Bimm stared up at him. His bright black eyes narrowed. "I will answer your questions in a moment, my young friend," he said in a low voice. "But first, you will have to answer mine."

Boba swallowed. His hand moved protectively toward his pocket. The Bimm's gaze followed it. Boba fingered the card in his pocket, but did not take it out.

He didn't have to. Nuri had already guessed what it was. He looked up at Boba. A smile filled the alien's broad face.

"Ah! I see!" said Nuri. "You have a filocard. You have come here to convert currency — or to get currency that you have stored in one of the banks here. May I see your card?"

Boba shook his head. His fingers tightened around the card in his pocket. He felt sweat beading on his forehead. What was the alien *really* after?

He glared at Nuri. He was still bigger than the alien. Stronger, too.

But then Boba remembered where he was: in a strange tunnel, on a strange planet. Even if he did escape from the Bimm, where would he go?

As though reading his mind, Nuri raised his hands. His expression was mild. "You misunderstand, young sir! I am no thief! I am here to provide a service, that is all. I can help you get your credits!"

The Bimm looked pointedly at Boba's pocket. A shining corner of the card stuck out. It glinted in the dim room.

"That is what I do," Nuri continued. "I help visitors. For a fee, of course."

Boba hesitated. If the alien tried to steal his card, Boba could knock him down. He could force the alien to do what *he* wanted.

Isn't that what bounty hunters did? Capture people?

Yet Nuri did not look dangerous. He looked

friendly. He looked like he really did want to help Boba. *To* — how had the Bimm put it? — *to provide a service.*

Could Boba trust him?

Boba remembered the dream he had about his father. *The* Dream.

"Trust no one, but use everyone."

Boba looked at the Bimm's bright, friendly eyes. Slowly he pulled the card from his pocket and nodded.

"Okay," he said. He held the card out. His own eyes were hard. "But remember — I'm a bounty hunter. Just like Aurra Sing. You wouldn't make her angry, right? Well, you don't want to even *think* about double-crossing me."

CHAPTER TEN

The Bimm stared at Boba. Then he bowed respectfully. "Of course, young sir. I am here to help you — for the fee I mentioned earlier."

Nuri took the card from Boba. The alien's fingers felt soft, furry, and very, very warm. Boba frowned slightly. "How much is the fee?"

Nuri held the card up to the soft yellow light of the passage. He examined it carefully. "That depends," he said.

Boba moved closer to him. He tried to figure out what the alien could see in the card. "Depends on what?"

"On how much this is worth." Nuri held up the card. "I can arrange for you to procure your currency, without, er, complications."

The alien glanced meaningfully at the door leading back out onto Level Two. Boba knew that by "complications," he meant Aurra Sing.

Boba asked, "How can you do that?"

Nuri shrugged. "By avoiding attention. As I am sure you have noticed, there are many rules on Aargau."

Boba nodded. "I saw that," he agreed.

"Well, some of us — many of us — have made our own rules. Now, I have shown trust in you, young sir, by telling you my name. But before I check this —" Nuri held up the shining card "— I must be able to trust *you*. I must know you are not dangerous, or a wanted man. I must know *your* name."

Boba nodded slowly, thinking.

He had to admit it. He liked the idea that someone thought him dangerous. It made him feel powerful. It made him feel that he had a secret.

Which, of course, he did. He knew that Count Tyranus and Count Dooku were the same person. That was a dangerous secret — but it gave him power.

And he was the only one who knew.

Also, of course, he *was* wanted — wanted by Aurra Sing!

Boba looked at Nuri. The Bimm still held his card up, waiting.

"My name," said Boba proudly, "is Boba Fett."

The Bimm stared at him. After a moment he

bowed. "Boba, sir," he said. "I am proud to meet you."

Boba bowed back, a little awkwardly. "And you — Nuri."

The Bimm straightened again. Suddenly he was all business.

"Now," Nuri said. He opened his pale yellow vest. Under it he wore a thick leather belt. On the belt was a small rectangular object: a computer of some sort.

Nuri fiddled with the computer, and it blinked to life. He held up the card, then inserted it into the top of the computer. The computer beeped and blinked. A small silvery screen lit up. There were numbers and letters on it which Boba could not understand.

Must be in Bimmsaarii, he thought.

Nuri peered down at the screen, reading it. His furry eyebrows raised in surprise. He looked up at Boba and said, "Well! You are quite a fortunate young bounty hunter, Boba, sir! You are worth a great deal."

Boba nodded. "I know."

"It says that this fortune was acquired for you by someone named Jango Fett," the Bimm went on. "Your father?"

"Yes," said Boba.

"Is he with you, then? He is the only other person allowed access to this treasure."

Boba shook his head. "N-no," he said. He could not keep the sorrow from creeping into his voice. "He's — he's not with me."

The Bimm looked up at him. His eyes were sympathetic and understanding. "I see," he said. He seemed to think for a minute, staring first at the card, then at Boba.

At last Nuri said, "This Aurra Sing. She is not someone I would want pursuing me. She has killed many people. Many powerful people. Here on Aargau, we are neutral. But we are not stupid. And we are not without sympathy for those in need."

He smiled at Boba, then held out the card for him to take. "Here, Boba, sir. I will help you retrieve your treasure. There will be a fee for my services, but you do not have to pay me in advance. I will deduct it from your card."

Boba looked at him. "Thank you," he said. He took the card and put it back into his pocket. "Could you tell which bank has the treasure in it?"

"No." Nuri rubbed his chin. "To get that information, you would have to go back to Level One, to the security desk."

Boba's heart sank. He looked at the door that led onto Level Two.

Somewhere out there, Aurra Sing was looking for him.

And, knowing Aurra Sing, she would find a way of obtaining a weapon — whether it was allowed or not.

Boba turned to Nuri. "Isn't there any other way?" he asked. "Besides going back up there?"

The little alien smiled. He put a reassuring hand on Boba's arm. "Boba, sir, I have told you that here on Aargau, some of us have made our own rules. Well, we have made our own place, too. A place where the other rules don't apply — and our rules do."

He turned and gestured toward the dim passage behind them. "I will take you to this place now, if you wish."

Boba looked at the Bimm, and then at the passage. He felt his neck begin to prickle with fear and excitement. "What is this place called?" he asked.

Nuri gazed down the passage and smiled — a strange, knowing smile.

"It is called," he said, "the Undercity."

CHAPTER ELEVEN

"The Undercity?" Boba echoed Nuri's words. "But —"

He stopped, remembering what he had been told on Level One.

You can find some very shady characters in the Undercity, the attendant had warned him. *It is terribly dangerous, especially with the recent skirmishes against the Separatists.*

And now Nuri wanted to take him there!

Just the thought scared Boba. But then he remembered what his father used to say —

Fear is energy, Jango had taught him. *And you can learn to control it. If you concentrate, you can change your energy, from fear to excitement. Then you can use that energy, instead of being used by it.*

Boba concentrated now. He closed his eyes. He could feel his heart pounding. He could feel his own fear.

He took a deep breath. He held it while he counted to three, then exhaled slowly.

This is energy, he thought. *And I can control it.* Breathe. Exhale.

Already he could feel his heart slowing down. Growing more calm. More in control.

Not afraid, but excited.

"Okay!" he said. He opened his eyes and saw Nuri a few feet ahead of him. "I'm ready! What are we waiting for?"

Nuri smiled. "This way," he said, and pointed down the passage.

Boba followed him. The passage twisted and turned. Tubes of glowing yellow lit their way. Now and then he saw small holosigns, covered with symbols he did not recognize. The images shifted and changed, from red to green to blue to purple. They made his eyes hurt to look at them. After a while he concentrated on staring at Nuri's back and nothing else.

After about five minutes the Bimm stopped. Set into the ground in front of him was a heavy, round, metal door. Nuri stooped and, with an effort, yanked the door open. He straightened, catching his breath, and stared at Boba.

"In a moment we will begin our descent to the lowest level of Aargau," Nuri said. "The actual surface of the planet. It is the remains of a vast city. It was built by the original natives of Aargau millions of years ago. The pyramid has grown out of it, layer by layer, level by level, over thousands of years. Aargau is a highly civilized planet now. As I told you, it has many rules. But it was not always so."

Here Nuri's expression grew serious. "In the Undercity, individuals are not as well-behaved as they are up here. It is dangerous to visit there. Sometimes fatal."

Boba swallowed. He tried to look brave — although he certainly didn't *feel* brave.

But that was okay. He felt excited. He was doing something he had never done before! And he was doing it on his own.

Well, almost. He looked at Nuri and smiled. "I can handle it," he said.

Nuri cocked his head. "You are not frightened?"

Boba shrugged. "Yeah. I am. But I haven't changed my mind. I still want to go."

Nuri looked pleased. "That is good. To admit fear is a good thing. It makes one careful. And carelessness has killed more visitors to the Undercity than anything else."

Nuri rubbed his chin, regarding Boba thoughtfully.

"And besides," said the little Bimm. His smile

grew even wider. "A visit to the Undercity is an important part of any bounty hunter's education!"

That made Boba feel good. He grinned back.

"Well then —" Nuri gestured at the opening in the floor in front of him. Boba took a deep breath, then stepped alongside him.

"I'm ready," he said, and looked down.

"Ready for anything?" asked Nuri.

Boba nodded. "Ready for anything!"

CHAPTER TWELVE

As Boba looked down, he saw what had been hidden behind the round door in the floor. A capsule, big enough to hold two people. It had clear sides, so you could see out of it. It had a control panel but no steering mechanism. It reminded him of the cloud car he had flown in Cloud City, only smaller, and with no way to change direction.

"What's that?" he asked.

Nuri bent to press a button on the capsule's side. Its top hatch opened. "Hop in and find out," he said.

Nuri climbed into the front. Boba slipped in behind him. The top closed again. Boba looked around and saw that the capsule was inside yet another tunnel — like a sort of tube, or slide, that curved and swirled and twisted ever downward.

"Is this how you get to the Undercity?" he asked.

Nuri nodded. "It is one of the ways. There are thousands. Many are only known to a handful of people. Many have been hidden for so long that they've been forgotten. Of course, there are *official* routes to the Undercity — turbolifts and such — but one needs special clearances for those. And money."

With no warning Nuri flicked a switch on the control board and the capsule plummeted downward with a sudden *whoosh*.

"Whoa!" Boba shouted. It was as though the entire floor had dropped away beneath them. The capsule shot almost straight down, then curved abruptly to the right. It corkscrewed around and around — like going down a gigantic, kilometers-long slide. Boba braced himself with his hands and looked out.

Everywhere he saw lights. Shimmering, blazing flashes of red and orange and blue and violet.

"Those are the other levels," Nuri explained. He had to shout to be heard over the rush and roar of their descent. "We are traveling at a rate of kilometers per minute — but in realtime, not in hyperspace."

"Cool!" said Boba. He wished this thing had controls!

He stared out again. He had glimpses of huge leaping flames, of tunnels that seemed to be filled with molten gold. One level was like a giant aquarium, where huge dianogas floated, their tentacles waving.

Boba wrinkled his nose. "Smells bad here," he said.

"Sanitation level," said Nuri. "We're almost there."

Suddenly everything went black. Not the kind of black you see at night when you go to sleep. Not the kind of black inside a closet, or a darkened ship. Not like the darkness of space, which was not darkness at all, but spangled with stars and planets and distant galaxies.

This was darkness like Boba had never seen. Like he had never imagined. It was like a huge, smothering hand pressed upon his face. Boba couldn't see Nuri in front of him. He couldn't see his own hand. For a heart-sickening second Boba imagined that he himself had disappeared. That he had somehow been transformed into antimatter. That he was —

"Here!" exclaimed Nuri.

An explosion of light surrounded them. Purple, green, deep blue. Boba blinked. The light flickered. It was not an explosion now, but flashes of color. Shapes. Buildings. Moving waves that were people. The familiar figures of droids, creatures, men, and women. Above them all was that terrible, strange darkness. It was like a cloud or a huge black curtain.

The capsule began to slow down. Boba let his breath out in relief. "That was great," he said. "Kind of creepy at the end, though."

Nuri nodded. "That was the emptiness between the Undercity and the upper levels. Sunlight never comes here. Only artificial light. And darkness."

Boba shivered. The capsule came to a halt. He gazed out at a teeming city. It was more crowded than anyplace he had ever seen. A disorderly mass of living things, more like a hive than anything else.

The capsule lid popped open. Nuri jumped out. He bowed to Boba.

"Welcome to the Undercity," he said.

Boba had thought that Level Two was crowded. He had thought that Coruscant was crowded, and the *Candaserri*, too.

None of these compared to the Undercity. There were so many people, so many beings, so many droids, so many *everything*, that his head whirled.

"Stay with me!" said Nuri. "If you get lost, you'll never find your way out."

Boba scowled. "Don't bet on that," he said. "I've got a good sense of direction."

"That might not be enough to help you here," replied Nuri.

Boba hated to admit it, but he had to agree with the Bimm. High above them, the sky that was not a sky was crisscrossed with thousands of shining objects. They looked like ribbons, or rainbows. But they were actually other chutes, or slides, like the one Boba had taken down here. He could see capsules speeding through them, up and down. The air was filled with bright airspeeders, swoop bikes, robo-hacks, even Podracers. On the ground, streets and sidewalks wound around tall, crumbling buildings. The streets were filled with rubbish, broken stones, mangled airspeeders.

And everywhere he looked, he saw people — nonhumans, mostly, but a lot of humans, too. None of them looked friendly. A lot of them looked dangerous.

"Hey, watch it!" someone snapped at Boba. A tall, angry-looking Caridian glared down at him.

"Sorry," said Boba. The Caridian jostled past him. Boba looked around: Nuri was gone!

Ulp. Boba swallowed. A group of swaggering space pirates went by him, laughing. Boba stared back at them, trying to look unimpressed.

"Young sir!" Nuri's voice carried from a few meters away. "This way!"

Boba hurried to join him. Past shops and markets, through abandoned structures that looked like ancient starships, under a vast broken glass dome. They passed food vendors, too. Some of what they were selling looked disgusting — things with claws and tentacles and too many eyes. But some of the food looked and smelled delicious. It made Boba's mouth water. He couldn't remember how long it had been since he had eaten. He was pretty sure it hadn't been today.

At first he tried to keep track of the way they were going. But after a while, Boba gave up trying to keep track. Their path wound in and out, back and forth. Once he was certain they were back-tracking. He wondered if for some reason Nuri was trying to fool him. Keep him from being able to find his way back on his own.

And no matter where they went, there were crowds. Despite the rule against nonnatives being armed, most of those he saw carried weapons of one sort or another. Vibroblades, stun batons, blasters, wrist rockets. Boba was pretty sure most of them *weren't* citizens of Aargau.

And he was pretty sure he would not want to bump into *any* of them, alone and unarmed.

"Where do all these people come from?" Boba asked.

Nuri led him down the street, toward an alley. "They come from all over the galaxy," he said in his high, singsong voice. "They are drawn by the fortunes to be made on Aargau, trading currency. And here in the Undercity, anything goes. Betrayal. Murder. The black market is busy here. Smugglers trade and sell gold, credits, data, droids, jewels, weapons, ships. But the single most valuable thing is *information*."

"Information?" Boba frowned. "That doesn't seem very interesting." *Not compared to weapons, or ships*, he thought.

"Trust me," said Nuri. "I know what I'm talking about. And stay near me — it's risky just coming down here. Especially for a first-timer."

I trust nobody, Boba thought angrily. At that instant, a figure rushed from the dark alley.

"Get back!" commanded Nuri.

"No!" said Boba. He reached for a broken brick to throw at the figure. It had nearly reached them, its arms outstretched. It was too dark to make it out clearly —

But not too dark to see that it was holding a blaster. And the blaster was pointed right at Boba Fett.

CHAPTER THIRTEEN

Boba swung his arm back, ready to hurl the brick. But before he could, Nuri stopped him.

"Stop!" the Bimm said. "Wait —"

The figure drew up beside them and halted, panting. It was a fur-covered Bothan, her pointy ears pressed back against her head in fear. "Nuri!" she exclaimed.

Nuri stared up at her in concern. "What is it, Hev'sin?" he asked.

"I have been searching for you!" She turned and looked at Boba. Her blaster was still pointed at him.

"Who is he?" she asked Nuri in a low, accusing voice.

Boba stared at his feet. Nuri glanced at him, then shook his head. "Only a boy," he said to the Bothan quietly. "You will not need your weapon with him. Tell me, Hev'sin — what is wrong?"

The Bothan hesitated. Then she slipped her blaster back into her belt. She stepped next to Nuri, and the two of them turned away slightly. It was obvious they were not worried about Boba overhearing them.

After all, Boba thought, *I'm only a boy. Not a serious threat.*

Or so you think.

Boba knew about Bothans. They were the greatest spies in the galaxy. They left their homeworld, Bothawai, and traveled everywhere. And everywhere they went, they found work — at undercover jobs, as independent operatives, or part of the Bothan Spynet.

And what was it Nuri had just said?

The single most valuable thing is information.

Boba pretended to stare at the alley nearby. But in fact he was listening to what the Bothan was saying.

Boba was spying.

Two can play this game, he thought. *And maybe only one can win — but that one will be me.*

He could hear Hev'sin talking, in a low, urgent voice. "They say he has come here to raise currency for the Separatists. That is why he is down in the Undercity. He is pretending to make a standard visit to the Banking Clan offices on Level Four, but his real business is down here. He doesn't want to draw the attention of members of the Republic."

"Are you sure of this, Hev'sin?" asked Nuri. He looked extremely interested, but not too alarmed.

"Positive," hissed the Bothan. "I saw him with my own eyes. He is surrounded by clone troopers — he never travels anywhere without a full guard now. Besides, I would know San Hill anywhere."

San Hill! Boba remembered — he had seen San Hill just a little while ago, up on Level Two — the man who was skinny and ugly as a stick insect. The Head of the InterGalactic Banking Clan.

San Hill was a Separatist. Boba learned this when he was on Geonosis, and he had seen San Hill meeting with Count Dooku. Boba wondered if San Hill knew that Dooku was the same person as Tyranus — Tyranus, who had created the clone troopers that were now attacking San Hill's allies!

I'll bet he doesn't *know*, thought Boba.

And then he had another thought.

Maybe he'd like *to know . . . for a price.*

Information was very valuable here on Aargau.

"Where did you see him?" Nuri was asking Bothan.

"Near the Hutts' gambling palace. You can be

certain San Hill is up to no good, if he is doing business with the Hutts."

Nuri nodded. "That is so."

Boba's eyes widened. *The Hutts!* He knew who they were — one of the most notorious clans in the galaxy! They ran smuggling and gambling houses all through Hutt Space, and beyond. Now it seemed that they had some sort of operation here on Aargau. An illegal one, too, since it was in the Undercity.

Boba's father, Jango, had done business with Jabba, the Hutt clan's ruler.

"The Hutts value a good bounty hunter," Jango had told his son. "They pay well, too — better than almost anyone."

For knowledge you must find Jabba, his father's book had said. Could Jabba the Hutt be here on Aargau?

Boba glanced over at Nuri and the Bothan, then quickly turned his head again.

"I must go now." The Bothan looked over her shoulder. She stared right past Boba. It was as though he was invisible to her. Another advantage of being young! "I knew you would want to know this, Nuri."

The Bimm nodded. "Yes. Thank you."

He handed her a coin. The Bothan looked at it,

disappointed. For a moment Boba thought she was going to argue — but then Boba remembered.

Bimms were expert hagglers.

And this Bothan didn't have time to waste on haggling. She gave Nuri a farewell that was more of a snarl, then turned and walked quickly away.

"Interesting," Nuri said, more to himself than Boba. "Most interesting."

He looked up, and it was as though he saw Boba for the first time. A small smile crossed the Bimm's face.

"Well, my young visitor," said Nuri. He gestured to the alley behind him. "Shall we go and get your money?"

Boba said nothing. He didn't move. Something about the Bimm seemed different. Maybe it was that smile. Maybe it was just that Boba was tired and hungry. He waited, and finally nodded.

"Okay," he said.

He followed Nuri into the alley. It was dim, but not too dark. It curved slightly, though, so Boba couldn't quite see what was ahead of him. A few more space pirates passed them, laughing loudly. Boba tried to stand as tall as he could when they walked by him. He'd give anything to be back on *Slave I*! He'd give anything to be off this planet, and on his own. . . .

"Here we are," said Nuri suddenly. He stopped in front of a metal door. There was a small window in the door, with bars in it. At the bottom was a narrow opening. Behind the barred window stood a very old, worn-out Admin droid.

"Can I help you?" it asked in a grating voice.

Nuri turned to Boba. "May I have your card, please?"

Boba thought for a moment. If the Bimm had meant to rob him, he could have done it before now. After a moment he shrugged. He pulled the card from his pocket and handed it to Nuri. The Bimm would still need Boba's DNA to get the credits.

Or would he?

"I'd like to have my fee deducted from this young man's account," said Nuri. He slid the card through the opening in the barred window. "Six hundred thousand mesarcs should do it."

The droid picked up the card. "As you wish," it said. It swiped the card across a shining red screen.

Boba watched the droid suspiciously. It hadn't bothered to question Boba at all. It hadn't even looked at him. And suddenly the words of the security attendant on Level One came back to him.

You must also be sure not to exchange your money from anyone who is not a licensed member of the Banking Clan. There are black-market money changers on Aargau.

This was an illegal banking machine.

"Hey!" yelled Boba. "What are you doing? That's *my* money!"

He lunged for the banking machine, jamming his hand through the narrow opening, reaching for the card and hitting at buttons to stop the transaction. He managed to halt things—but it was already too late.

"Five hundred thousand mesarcs have been taken from your account," the droid said in its rusty voice. It dropped the card back into the opening. "Have a nice day."

Boba grabbed the card. He turned furiously to Nuri.

"You!" Boba began to shout. But then he stopped.

Nuri was morphing. His face went from yellow fur to silver to green. He grew taller, his arms grew longer, until he towered above Boba.

He wasn't a Bimm at all.

"You're a shapeshifter!" gasped Boba.

CHAPTER FOURTEEN

"You're a clever young man," the Clawdite shapeshifter said. It was a *young* shapeshifter, with a menacing, oozing voice. Its body seemed to melt and re-form before Boba's eyes. Its body took on muscle, sinew, strength. Its head grew dark thick hair. Its eyes grew dark as well.

"But not quite clever enough," it said.

Boba stared at it in amazement. "But —"

"Consider yourself lucky, young sir," said the shapeshifter that had been Nuri. "I could have taken your precious card and kept it all for myself. I could have killed you."

The shapeshifter smiled — the same unpleasant smile Boba had last seen on the Bimm's face.

"But I admire your courage," the Clawdite went on. "You're young and learning, just like me. And I hate Aurra Sing. She is my rival. It seems you and I have that in common. I could have left you up on Level Two. She would have found you there, very soon. But finding you would have pleased Aurra Sing. I hate her far too much for that."

Boba stared furiously at the Clawdite. "You have no right to claim what's mine!"

The Clawdite laughed. "Well, you did take the card out before I could get everything. If you can somehow find your way back to the Upper Levels, you will find there is enough money left for you to buy a way to get off-planet. But only if you are clever enough, Boba. You will have to avoid being found by Aurra Sing. You will have to find a way to the Upper Levels. And then you will have to find your way to what's left of your inheritance."

The Clawdite tilted his head. "I said that the Undercity is part of any bounty hunter's education. I know it's a big part of mine. I hope you have enjoyed your lesson, Boba."

And with a mocking bow, the Clawdite turned and hurried down the alley.

Boba stared after him. *How could I have been so careless?* he thought angrily. *I forgot the number one rule of bounty hunters —*

Trust no one.

The Bimm — no, the *Clawdite* — had betrayed him. Still, the shapeshifter was right. Boba had learned an important lesson. Next time he wouldn't be so quick to accept help.

If there *was* a next time.

But what to do now? Boba turned and looked at the droid behind its barred window. Hmmm. Nuri had been able to get money from Boba's account. Why not Boba himself? He walked over to the window.

"I'd like to get the rest of my money," he said. He slipped the card through the opening.

The droid looked at him with its unblinking eyes. It took the card and slid it into a slot in its arm. "Sorry," it said. "You do not have permission to use this terminal."

It slipped the card back to Boba. Clearly, the Clawdite had known an access code that Boba couldn't even guess at.

"What?" Boba said angrily. "You mean —"

"Sorry," said the droid. "Shall I call security to assist you?"

"No," Boba said hastily. He began to walk away.

Then he stopped. Before, when the Clawdite had given Boba's card to the droid, the robot had said something — something about a bank.

Boba still had the card. If he knew exactly where his money was, he could get it himself — without Aurra Sing!

He went quickly back to the window. "What bank did you say that money was in?"

The droid tilted its shining chromium head. "InterGalacticBank of Kuat. Level Two. Shall I call security to assist you?"

"No!" Boba said quickly. "I mean, no thanks!"

Nuri had been right — information *was* valuable!

But he had no time to celebrate his good luck. Behind him came the sound of footsteps and more harsh laughter. Boba looked back and saw several tall, heavily armed figures. More pirates, no doubt.

Time to get out of here! He turned and ran soundlessly down the alley.

It ended on another street. This was one was even busier and more crowded than those he'd been on earlier, with Nuri. Boba stood for a minute, catching his breath. He felt no fear whatsoever. He felt anger, and excitement, and determination. He wasn't too worried about Aurra Sing down here. What were the odds of her finding him in all this chaos?

Still, where should he go?

He looked up and down the street. As far as he could see in every direction, there were shops. Some were brightly lit and filled with bustling service droids and well-dressed humanoids and aliens. Others were dim, with only one or two grim figures standing guard by the entrance. Some were in buildings that were little more than piles of rubble. All seemed to be gambling dens of some sort. Many had signs that blinked or scrolled messages in brilliant green or gold or silver letters.

ALL CURRENCIES CHANGED HERE
ALL COIN ACCEPTED
NO SUM TOO SMALL!

Boba began to walk. Excited, noisy crowds spilled from doorways into the street around him. Robo-hacks — airborne taxis — hovered in front of gambling houses, waiting to take new customers away to spend the riches they had just won. Evil-looking figures lurked in alleyways, waiting to pounce on unsuspecting passersby. High above, the air was crisscrossed with glowing tubes. Shining capsules sped up and down between the Undercity and the Upper Levels. In between, swoop bikes and airspeeders flashed.

That's what I'm going to get! Boba thought as he watched a swoop bike whoosh by. Once he figured out how to get his money, maybe he could hire one to take him back to *Slave I* — although flying one himself would be better!

"Pagh! Human scum! Out of my way!" a voice snarled.

Boba looked up, startled. A figure blocked the street before him. It was tall, with orange eyes in a pale fungoid-looking face, and a long trunklike appendage wrapped around its throat. A Twi'lek.

"Didn't you hear me?" the Twi'lek repeated fiercely. Its hand moved threateningly beneath its robes.

"Sorry," Boba said hastily. He stepped aside. The Twi'lek gave him a sneering look, then pushed him aside and strode past him. Boba watched him go, thinking.

"Wait a minute," he said softly to himself.

He had an idea!

His father had told him once about a Twi'lek named Bib Fortuna. The grub-faced alien had served as Jabba the Hutt's right hand, helping run his gambling operations on Tatooine and other places across the galaxy. Here on Aargau there was a Hutt gambling palace. Was there a chance that *this* Twi'lek was the one his father meant?

Boba stared after the retreating figure. If it *was* Bib Fortuna, he might be heading toward the Hutt's den.

Boba knew the odds were against it — but then, everyone in the Undercity seemed willing to gamble. He'd take a chance.

Boba began to hurry after the Twi'lek. He was

careful to stay out of sight and to always keep him in his view. Sometimes this was hard, as the alien ducked in and out of narrow alleys and tunnels. Still, Boba followed him tirelessly through the maze that was the Undercity.

Check this out, Boba thought with a grin. He was stalking his prey through incredibly dangerous terrain — just like a bounty hunter!

CHAPTER FIFTEEN

The Twi'lek had reached the end of a long, narrow winding street. He halted in front of a large building with a rounded roof that had spikes on it. The building was shaped like the head of a gigantic krayt dragon. The dragon's open mouth was the door. Inside, Boba could see a bustling throng of aliens, humans, and droids. Between the krayt dragon's teeth, a shimmering holosign flashed green-and-gold Huttese letters.

The Twi'lek walked up to the sign. Without hesitating, it went inside.

Boba watched him go. His heart was beating hard now. He had seen a lot of people, a lot of aliens, and a lot of droids since he'd been in the Undercity. But there was one thing he *hadn't* seen.

He hadn't seen a single kid. He hadn't seen a single person his own age.

The last thing he wanted to do was draw attention to himself. Silence and stealth were a bounty hunter's greatest weapons.

But there was no way he could sneak through that krayt's mouth and into the gambling palace unnoticed. A bunch of burly guards stood just inside the entrance — Gamorrean boars, by the look of them. Boba watched as the Twi'lek strode right past them. They bowed to him slightly, but otherwise paid him no notice. Yet when two Wookiees approached moments later, the Gamorrean guards frisked them before waving them inside.

How could Boba get past them?

Boba glanced behind him, down the winding street. He could see two more groups of people heading toward the Hutts' gambling palace. If he remained where he was, he'd be seen. At best he'd be told to leave. At worst —

He couldn't afford to think of that now. A few yards away, a pile of rubble loomed. Quickly, before the approaching groups could see him, Boba ran and ducked beside it.

The first group grew nearer. Boba could see them clearly now: half a dozen small Jawa scavengers. All wore the Jawas' distinctive hooded robes. All spoke to one another in the Jawas' usual babble. As they passed, their eyes glowed from within their hoods like tiny torches.

"Hey," whispered Boba to himself.

He had another idea — a good one.

He turned and quickly began searching through the rubble. Bricks, broken glass, shreds of leather. A melted ruin that had once been a blaster. Broken spear-points. Exploded grenades. Something that looked alarmingly like a human hand.

The Hutts' gambling palace was a popular place. But it probably wasn't a good idea to stick around it too long.

Suddenly, Boba found what he was looking for. He bit his lip to keep from crying aloud in triumph. It was only a rag — a long, grayish-yellow piece of cloth, dirty and full of holes.

But it was good enough for him. Boba glanced back to make sure no one had sighted him. The Jawas were just approaching the entrance now. One of them appeared to be talking to the Gammorean guards. Swiftly, Boba pulled the cloth over his head. It smelled bad — it stank, as a matter of fact — but he gritted his teeth and tried to arrange it properly.

He pulled part of it over his face. He tugged it forward, till it covered his face like a hood. The cloth fell to just below his knees. He removed his belt from his tunic and tied it loosely around his waist. That was better. He was a little taller than the Jawas, so he bent his knees. It was hard to walk that way, but once he was inside, maybe no one would notice if he straightened up.

He peered around the pile of rubble. Another group was nearing the gambling palace. They were too far away for him to see clearly, but they were tall, and vaguely humanoid.

And there were a lot of them.

I'd better get inside, fast.

Boba looked down at the gambling palace. The Gammorean guards were nodding and waving the Jawas inside. Boba waited until the last Jawa had disappeared into the krayt dragon's mouth. Then he took a deep breath, and began to hurry toward the entrance.

But when he got there he stopped. One of the Gammorean guards glared down at him, grunting in a questioning tone. It held a tall spear, and waved it menacingly.

Its partner peered through its piggy little eyes at Boba, skeptical.

Boba bent his knees a little more. He tugged the folds of cloth around his head, praying his face didn't show. He pointed toward the entrance, miming that he wanted to go inside.

Just then, one guard nudged the other, grunting and pointing behind Boba.

"Aarrrgh!" snarled the other guard. It gnashed its tusks angrily and stared where the other had indicated.

Boba wanted to turn and look behind him — but he didn't dare. He stood, wondering if he should make a dash for the entrance.

Without warning, one of the Gammoreans swung his spear through the air high above Boba's head. He gestured Boba inside.

Boba nodded eagerly. Gathering the folds of his cloak, he ducked his head, then walked as fast as he could through the krayt dragon's mouth — and into the domain of the Hutts.

CHAPTER SIXTEEN

Inside the gambling palace, the noise was deafening. Laughter, angry shouts, howls of triumph and disappointment — all mingled with the jingle of coins, the rattle of dice, the clack of Kenoballs, the cries of card dealers and money changers. The Hutts' gambling palace was yet another maze, all smoke-filled rooms and arcades, so crowded with gamblers that Boba could hardly squeeze through. Gamorrean boars lumbered around, keeping order and throwing out the most unruly customers. Boba saw the Jawas he'd seen outside, haggling with a Bimm over a game of Outlander. Boba wondered if it was a real Bimm or another shapeshifter.

"Watch the Podraces!" a voice shouted. Boba looked up and saw a huge screen. Podraces were being broadcast from Tatooine. "No bets refused!"

Boba fingered the card in his pocket. He was too smart to waste his money on betting. His father had warned him against gambling.

"A bounty hunter gambles with his life every day," Jango always said. "Only a fool would gamble with money, too."

Boba tugged his ragged hood closer around his face. He had only one aim now — to find some way back to the Upper Levels. To find some way of locating his treasure. To get back to *Slave I* and leave Aargau — without Aurra Sing.

He put his hand in his pocket and touched the book his father had left him.

For knowledge you must find Jabba.

Find Jabba. Boba had always assumed that to locate the notorious gangster, he would have to go to Jabba's homeworld of Nal Hutta. Or to Tatooine, where the powerful clan leader had created a smuggling empire.

But what if Jabba were here, on Aargau? The Hutts were involved in every kind of illegal activity in the galaxy. Maybe Jabba was actually here, in the Undercity — in this very gambling palace!

But how to find him? Boba thought hard. He'd have to find the Twi'lek again — the one he thought might be the famous Bib Fortuna. He pulled the ragged cloak back a little from his eyes, straining to see through the dim, smoky room.

A deep voice snarled behind him. Boba looked

up and saw one of the Gamorrean boars. A spear was raised threateningly in his huge hand. The message was clear. *If you're not spending money, get out of here!*

Boba nodded apologetically. He started to turn away, when the guard suddenly grabbed his shoulder.

Ulp! If the guard pulled off his disguise, there'd be no Boba, either! Quickly he dug into his pocket and held up his card, careful to hold it in his sleeve, so his hand wouldn't show. It flickered gold in the dim light.

The Gamorrean's ugly pig face grew even uglier with disappointment. With a grunt the guard turned away and began to hassle someone else.

Whew, thought Boba. *That was close. Got to be more careful!*

He began edging through the crowd, looking for the Twi'lek. Once he thought he saw him, but it turned out to be a tall alien wearing a fur coat. Once he thought he heard a Wookiee's deep, hooting voice. But it turned out to be a small armored droid, rolling through the crowd.

Boba watched it curiously. Then he looked around. There were a *lot* of droids here — more than he would have expected.

Why were they here?

As he looked around, he noticed that these weren't protocol droids, or service droids. They weren't servomechs, either.

They were sentry droids. And security droids, and powerful police droids. Boba felt the skin on his neck prickle. He glanced up, and saw a guard droid hovering on the other side of the room. It turned slowly in the air, its sensors scanning the den. Its three weaponry arms were poised to fire if necessary.

"What's going on?" Boba whispered. Whatever it was, he didn't like it or trust it — one bit.

As if in answer to his thoughts, two tall women in pilot uniforms passed him. They were talking in low voices. Boba pulled his ragged cloak around his face and turned away. But he was listening.

"Rumor is that Dooku sent him," one of the pilots said quietly. "Raising more funds."

"There aren't enough credits in the galaxy to overthrow the Republic," the other woman retorted. "Dooku is mad."

"I assure you, that is the one thing he is not," countered her friend. "And there may not be enough money in the galaxy to fund a rebellion — but there certainly is enough in the Hutts' pockets!"

The women pilots laughed softly. They walked around a corner, out of Boba's earshot.

Count Dooku! Could the sinister Count be here as well?

No — the pilot had said, *Dooku sent him.*

Who would the Count have sent?

Boba thought fast. And he remembered.

San Hill. The head of the InterGalactic Banking Clan, and one of the most powerful figures in the galaxy. But just a little while ago the Bothan spy had told Nuri that San Hill was here, in the Under-city —

San Hill was raising funds for the Separatists. Raising money for Count Dooku. And at the same time, the clone troopers were here as a security force of the Republic — clone troopers who had been bred at the command of Tyranus.

The two sides were set to oppose each other, Republic and Separatists. Clones and droids. But behind each side was the same person: the man Boba knew as the Count.

Count Tyranus.

Count Dooku.

It was all part of some terrible plot, Boba was sure of that. He was also sure that, if his father were still alive, he would find a way to make use of this information — especially with San Hill on the same planet.

Boba could make use of it, too. He just had to

figure out how. Maybe the pilots would have more information. He turned and began to move stealthily after them, across the crowded floor.

But when Boba turned the corner, the pilots were gone. Instead, he found himself face-to-face with three tall, vicious figures. Armorlike scales covered their bodies, and their broad, lipless mouths were full of sharp teeth. Long tails protruded from beneath their tunics, lashing the air threateningly as they argued and laughed in deep, throaty voices.

Reptilian Barabels!

"Care to join us?" one hissed at Boba. They were in the middle of a game of three-handed solitaire. "The stakes are high, Jawa — your money, or your life!"

The Barabel jabbed at him with one long, pointed claw, and the others laughed.

Boba shook his head. He began to back away. But before he could, fast as lightning, the Barabel's clawed hand grabbed him by the shoulder. Boba ducked, kicking out at the Barabel's ankle. The tall reptile gave a shout of rage and pain. He snatched his hand back, his claws closing tightly around Boba's ragged cloak. Boba dove for the floor. The cloak hung from the Barabel's claws like a ribbon of gray mist.

"That's no Jawa!" one of the other Barabels hissed.

That's right, thought Boba grimly. He rolled across the floor, landed on his stomach, and immediately pulled himself under a table. Above him the Barabels stared at the ragged cloak. They all looked around, nostrils flaring as they peered in vain for Boba.

Meanwhile, Boba hunched back as far as he could into the darkness beneath the table and held his breath. One of the Barabels shook its heavy, lizardlike head. He snorted, snatched the ragged cloak from his friend and tossed it over his shoulder.

"Forget about him! Scavenging scum! Back to the game!"

Once again, the Barabels clustered together, jaws clacking as they looked hungrily over the cards in their hands.

Boba let out a sigh of relief. He was safe.

For the moment . . .

CHAPTER SEVENTEEN

He rested for only a few minutes.

Now what? he thought. He no longer had his disguise. If he tried to move, he'd be spotted and thrown out of the gambling palace. Probably his card would be confiscated, too. Then he'd be on his own, with no money and no way out of the Undercity.

And that was the *best* that might happen.

The worst was that he'd be killed. Or captured by slavers.

Boba clenched his jaw grimly. That would never happen. He wouldn't *let* it happen. A good bounty hunter never gets caught.

And he was going to be one of the best.

Still, he needed a plan. *If* he could find the Twi'lek — *if* the Twi'lek really was Bib Fortuna — it might lead him to Jabba the Hutt. *If* Jabba the Hutt was actually here — and *if* the gangster would help him get back up to Level Two.

That's a lot of ifs, thought Boba.

He began to crawl toward the other side of the table. From down here, the Hutts' gambling palace was a forest of legs. Boba scanned the room for a pair of legs that belonged to a Twi'lek. He didn't see them — but he saw something else.

On the far side of the room, in a shadowy alcove, a familiar shadowy form stood, arms crossed. The figure was clad in a tight-fitting crimson suit. Its long legs were encased in high brown leather boots. A leather weapons vest covered its chest. Its skin glowed dead-white even in the darkness of the gambling den. A long topknot of brilliant red hair cascaded down its back. Blazing blue eyes scanned the room, missing nothing. Seeing everything.

Aurra Sing.

Boba's heart raced. He had imagined things couldn't get worse — but they just had. There *was* one thing worse than being captured or killed — and that was being captured or killed by the galaxy's most vengeful bounty hunter. Aurra Sing would show no mercy. She wouldn't care that he was a kid, or Jango Fett's son. To her, he was a double-crosser. Someone who'd cheated her out of her share of the fortune — even if the fortune wasn't rightly hers.

Well, this was no time to *stop* deceiving her. Boba watched as Aurra continued to scan the room. Abruptly, she spun on her heel and began walking — right toward where he crouched beneath the table.

Boba held his breath and froze. He watched as the supple brown boots strode past him — just inches from his nose. A few feet away they came to a stop. He heard the hiss of the Barabels whispering in their own language. Then he heard Aurra's low, powerful voice.

"I'm looking for a boy," she said. "About this tall. Brown hair, brown eyes. Wearing a blue tunic and black boots — though he might be in disguise. I wouldn't put it past him," she added grudgingly.

"We've seen no one," a Barabel hissed. "Now leave us, unless you wish to join our — *ach*!"

Boba edged forward, just enough to peek out. One of Aurra Sing's powerful hands was wrapped tightly around the Barabel's throat. Her other hand held a dagger warningly before her.

"I'm not here to waste my time with filth like you," she spat. "Answer! Have you seen a boy?"

"Yesssss," hissed the Barabel. His clawed hand gestured wildly. "Minutes ago — right there —"

Boba sucked his breath in sharply. There was no time to lose. He turned and scrambled toward the back of the table. A wall was there — solid wood. Boba felt around on the floor, searching for a weapon — a stick, a brick, anything he might use to defend himself. His hand closed on something cold and hard. A heavy metal ring, bigger than his hand. He pulled at it as hard as he could. It weighed a ton, but he kept pulling, until at last it moved.

To his shock, the floor moved, too. Boba stared down in astonishment.

The ring was bolted to the floor. It was not a ring, but a handle. When he had tugged at it, he had lifted a panel off the floor.

It was a trapdoor.

"You better not be lying." Aurra Sing's harsh voice rang across the room from just meters away. "Otherwise I'll carve new scales on your ugly faces."

Boba heard footsteps — Aurra's feet, heading toward the table. He pulled harder at the ring, try-ing to pry the entire panel up from the floor. The steps grew closer. The wood squeaked and grated as the panel edged up. The sound seemed deafen-ing to Boba. Now the panel was a few centimeters above the floor. He slid his hands beneath, and with all his strength pushed it up, up, until there was a space large enough for him to squeeze through. He shoved his feet in, kicking wildly at open air.

What if there were no floor? What if the trapdoor opened onto — nothing?

"All right, kid — this is it!" Aurra's gloating voice echoed from the room directly above him.

Boba took one last deep breath. He forced his legs through the trapdoor, then his chest and his shoulders. He slid down, his hands holding the wood panel above him. Beneath him he felt nothing, just raw empty space, black as the air above the Undercity. For an endless horrible moment he hung there, suspended between the floor above and nothing below. Then, with a gasp, he tugged the floor board back into place. It shut without a sound. His fingers slipped from the bare wood. His arms flailed at the air. And without a sound, Boba fell.

CHAPTER EIGHTEEN

It seemed he fell forever in that close, hot darkness. In reality, it was just seconds.

"*Ow.*" With a dull thud, he hit the ground. For a moment he lay there, catching his breath. He stared up. Perhaps three meters above him, he could just make out a black square bounded by four thin, weakly shining lines.

The trapdoor.

Would Aurra notice it? Boba wasn't going to wait and find out. Very carefully he stood, blinking as his eyes tried to adjust to the darkness. From overhead he could hear the sounds of the Hutts' den, somewhat muffled now. As his eyes grew accustomed to the dark, he found that he could see a little bit. The faint light from around the trapdoor showed him that he was in a tunnel. It stretched before him and behind him. He turned and peered into the blackness.

Which way should he go?

Above him he heard the scrape of booted feet upon the floor.

Aurra.

Boba chose to go forward — and fast. As quickly and carefully as he dared, he walked, his hands held before him. Now and then he shuddered as something dank and stringy touched his face or hands.

Cobwebs — at least, he *hoped* they were just cobwebs. Sometimes he thought he heard something skittering underfoot, a dry, rasping sound as of many tiny legs. And after several minutes of feeling his way through the dark, he heard something else as well.

Voices.

They came from somewhere ahead of him. Boba noticed that the tunnel seemed to be growing lighter. Instead of blackness, he was now surrounded by dark gray, like smoke. And now he could see that there were other tunnels branching off from this one. All stretched off into utter blackness. From some of them faint scurrying and chittering sounds echoed.

Boba shivered. If he had taken one of those paths by mistake, he might have wandered down here forever. He didn't want to think about what might live in them. And behind him he heard no footsteps following. There was no sign that Aurra Sing had come after him. He had managed to escape her again.

Maybe his luck was holding out, after all.

The light came from straight ahead, directly in front of him. Boba hurried toward it. He was so intent on getting there that he did not hear the soft clatter of many tiny feet in the tunnel behind him.

Just a few feet before him the passage abruptly ended. A pale square of light glowed on the floor. Boba looked down, and saw a small grille set into the ground at his feet. Through it he could make out dim shapes in a room below him.

"You are certain we are safe here?" a voice asked in the room below.

"Absolutely," a very deep, slow voice responded. It laughed, a horrible, hollow sound. "Hoh, hoh! My uncle himself has seen that this place is secure. No one can get here without our knowledge."

Boba's eyes widened. He was gazing into a secret chamber! The grille must have been put there to aid in spying. Boba slowly lowered himself, until he was kneeling and peering over the very edge of the grille. He was careful to stay back, in case someone happened to look up at the ceiling.

"That is good," the first voice said. Boba blinked. After the darkness of the long tunnel, it was hard to get used to the light again. But after a few seconds he could see more clearly.

And what he saw made his breath catch in surprise.

In the room below, a tall, skeletally thin figure sat in a large chair. To either side of him, armed guards stood. They were not clone guards, or droids, either. These were muscular humanoid figures, in drab gray uniforms with blasters slung at their sides. The figure they guarded was San Hill.

"It is in your uncle's interest to support our cause," said the head of the Banking Clan. "Count Dooku has assured me of that."

Boba had to squint to get a good look at the other figure in the room. It was big — huge in fact. A vast, mounded, sluglike body, reclining upon an even vaster chair like a throne. It had tiny, weak-looking arms and a long, fat tail. Layers of fat cascaded beneath its wide, froglike mouth. It was surrounded by guards as well. Boba swallowed nervously.

Was this Jabba the Hutt? If so, he was even more disgusting than his father had described him as being.

The sluglike creature shook its head. "My uncle will make up his own mind," he said in his booming voice. "He will not be hurried, even by Count Dooku."

"Why is your uncle not here?" asked San Hill in a soothing but irritated tone. He looked angry and impatient. "I wish to do business with Jabba himself, not some underling!"

"Gorga is not an underling!" boomed the Hutt. His tiny arms beat against his vast slimy chest. "My uncle is busy tending to our interests on Tatooine. If you desire, you may visit him there. But I would advise against it," Gorga added with a long, rolling laugh.

Boba grimaced. So this was Jabba's nephew! He had a hard time imagining something more repulsive than Gorga. But it seemed like he would have to, until he could see Jabba himself.

Boba felt a stab of disappointment and nervousness. He had hoped that Jabba would be here, to give him the advice — the knowledge — that his father had said the old crimelord possessed.

But Jabba was not here. He was on Tatooine.

I have to get to Slave I, Boba thought grimly. *I have to get to Tatooine.*

He had wasted enough time here in the Undercity. He had the information he needed about his father's fortune. It was in the Kuat Bank vaults on

Level Two. He had his card. *Slave I* was waiting for him, back on Level One. All he had to do was get to the bank, get his credits, and he would have enough to get off of Aargau, and on to Tatooine.

Just the thought of flying again made Boba feel better. He would trace his way back through the tunnel, back to the trapdoor. He'd figure out a way to open it again and climb out. Then he'd figure out how to get back to Level Two. He'd come this far on his own, right?

He could do it.

As silent as a shook, Boba began to inch away from the grill. Then he turned and started running back up the tunnel. It curved and curved, and once more Boba saw all those side passages, black and yawning like huge mouths.

Don't look at them. Keep your eyes on the tunnel!

Ahead he could just make out the sliver of light that fell from the trapdoor. He began to run even faster —

And suddenly, he stopped.

"No!" he whispered.

In the middle of the passage, something was crawling toward him. It was more than a half-meter long, with many black, jointed legs and a long, jointed body. Two long, clacking pincers were raised above its mandibles. Its small beady red eyes were fixed on Boba, and its jaws clashed together as it skittered toward him.

A kretch!

Boba kicked at it. He heard its claws clack, then felt them brush against his leg as it lunged for him. He jumped to one side, but the kretch was too fast — it followed, brushing up against his boot.

Boba kicked it again. This time he felt a satisfying *thump* as his foot connected with the scorpion-like creature. The kretch went flying, and with a loud crack struck the tunnel wall.

But now Boba heard more sounds — other small, clacking creatures skittering up the passage.

He turned to race toward the trapdoor —

And ran right into a tall figure. It was a man, wearing the same drab gray uniform as the guards he had seen surrounding San Hill in Gorga's hideaway.

But this man was no guard or underling. He wore the dress uniform of a high-ranking official in San Hill's employ, a broad decorative belt, and an expression that was equal parts suspicion and command. He smiled grimly down at Boba.

"Going somewhere?" he asked.

CHAPTER NINETEEN

Boba stared at the official in dismay. Behind him the kretch insects chattered and clacked. He glanced down at them. Then he grabbed Boba by the arm, turned, and pressed his own hand against the wall. Immediately, a hidden door opened. The official pulled Boba after him. The door closed as the kretch insects hissed and chittered, furious at losing their prey.

"So." The man gazed down thoughtfully at Boba. "It seems we *do* have a spy in our midst. But not a very careful one. Let's get a look at you."

He shone a torch into Boba's face. The boy shaded his eyes with his hand as the man stooped to stare at Boba intently. He had long, reddish hair, a rugged face. A jagged scar ran from below one eye, across his cheek and to his chin.

"Who are you?" Boba ventured.

"Vice-chair Kos of galactic accounts," the official replied. He held Boba's chin in his hand. Boba stared back at him defiantly, saying nothing. The man continued to look at him. Finally Kos shook his head. His eyes narrowed, as his expression changed.

"I know what you are," he said. "You're that Clawdite spy we heard about." A slight, almost admiring, smile creased his face. "Disguised as a boy — very clever."

Boba began to shake his head no. Then he stopped.

A Clawdite shapeshifter could look like anyone, or anything his size. The vice-chair thought he was Nuri!

"That's right," said Boba slowly. He looked warily up at the official.

The man's smile hardened. "Well, San Hill has his own methods of dealing with spies." He began to pull Boba toward him.

"And so does my master," said Boba.

Kos stopped. He stared at Boba suspiciously. "What do you mean by that?"

Boba hesitated. He had the kind of information a spy would have — real, possibly deadly, information. Out of everyone here on Aargau — out of everyone in the galaxy — only Boba knew that the Count was playing a deadly game. The Count was pretending to be two people, on opposing sides of a great, galaxy-spanning conflict.

It was information worth staking one's life on. And right now, that's what Boba was going to do.

"San Hill only knows part of the story," said Boba. He tried to keep his voice calm.

"And you know the rest?" snapped the vice-chair. But he looked uneasy. He glanced over his shoulder, then drew Boba close to him. "What have you heard?" Kos asked in a whisper. His gloved hands held Boba so tightly the boy's arm ached. "There have been rumors, a thousand rumors."

Boba's heart hammered inside his chest. He was in great danger — but with danger comes opportunity. If he was clever, he could use this official to escape from the Undercity; maybe even to escape from Aargau. . . .

"I know nothing of rumors," Boba said at last. He held his head up proudly and gazed straight into the vice-chair's eyes. "I know only the truth — but the truth comes at a price."

Kos stared fixedly at Boba. He seemed to be weighing his choices.

"I don't have all day," said Boba. "And neither do those I serve." He looked knowingly past the vice-chair, as though he saw someone else there.

Kos stiffened. His hand touched his weapons

belt, as though for reassurance. "Your price?" he said. "Your miserable shapeshifting skin should be price enough! You tell me what you know, and I'll let you go free — for now."

Boba fought to keep his voice steady. He could sense Kos's fear — if Boba could control his own fear, *he* would have the upper hand. "No. That's not enough. I will share my information — but first you have to bring me to Level Two."

"Level Two?" The vice-chair started laughing. Then his laughter turned to restrained fury. "I could break your neck right here — but after San Hill hears your news, he will devise more entertaining ways to kill you."

"After they hear my news," said Boba softly, "he will kill *you* for not taking me to him sooner. But by then my master will be here, and . . ."

He let his voice trail off threateningly.

The official stared at him. His face grew dark with anger. His hand moved toward Boba's neck.

Boba took a deep breath. If he was going to die right now, he would die fighting. He gazed unafraid and defiant up at his captor.

But then Kos stopped. He looked at the boy. His scarred face seemed to regard Boba with more re-spect. At last he nodded.

"All right," he said. "We'll do it your way. Trouble is brewing, that's for sure. Might as well be out of this place when the storm breaks."

He pushed Boba roughly ahead of him. There was the click of a blaster being loosed from its holster. "But don't even dream of escaping. I'll bring you to Level Two —"

"To the Kuat Bank," said Boba quickly.

For a moment the guard was silent. Then he laughed. "Kuat, eh? Well, someone must be paying you well for your services. But I guess you must be worth it, eh?"

You don't know the half of it, Boba thought, as the lieutenant marched him down the dark passage.

CHAPTER TWENTY

They walked in near-darkness for what seemed like hours, the torch's beam guiding them. But in reality, only a short while had passed — Boba had to remind himself that the darkness was deceptive, like everything else on Aargau.

At last they reached a spot where the tunnel widened. In front of them was a wide metal door. And in front of the door was an airspeeder.

"Get in," Kos snapped. He kept his blaster trained on Boba.

Boba clambered inside. He couldn't keep from smiling. Just the sight and feel of a cockpit made his blood race with excitement!

"What are you grinning at?" the official said suspiciously.

Boba composed his face into a calmer expression. "I am thinking that you made the right choice," he said.

This seemed to satisfy the vice-chair. He climbed into the pilot's seat, positioned himself behind the controls, and pressed a button. The wide door slid up, revealing a huge empty airshaft. It stretched up into dark, seemingly limitless space. Boba craned his neck and stared up.

Not limitless. High, high above them he could see a glitter of green.

"A shortcut," said the vice-chair. He allowed himself a smile. "This ventilation shaft opens directly onto Level Two. And — lucky for you! — the Kuat vaults are not far at all."

Without warning he grabbed the controls. The power generator roared to life. With a shudder the airspeeder bucked forward. Then, as Kos hit the throttle, the craft zoomed straight up.

Boba grabbed hold of his seat. This was more like it! He eyed the airspeeder's controls longingly. The craft rocked back and forth. It rose so quickly Boba's ears hurt from the abrupt change in air pressure. He looked aside at Kos piloting the craft.

I could fly this thing better than he can, Boba thought disdainfully.

Still, he had to admit, the vice-chair did go fast. Mere minutes passed, as they flew up, up, up.

Sooner than Boba could have imagined, the speeder came to a halt.

"Well then," said Kos. The speeder hovered in the air of the shaft. A few feet away was a wall, and a door with a sign on it.

LEVEL TWO, it read in glowing green letters.

A small metal platform extended from the door, hanging out over empty space. Boba turned and looked behind him. More emptiness. He looked up, squinting in the darkness.

He could barely make it out, but there it was. Far above him was a faint red shimmer: Level One. He looked down. He gulped. They must be miles and miles above the Undercity.

"Now." Kos turned to Boba. His eyes had grown even more intent, even more menacing. "You see that door there? I will open it, and allow you to enter Level Two — but not until you tell me what you know."

Boba's gaze shifted from the man to the platform. If he jumped from the airspeeder, he might be able to make it. But even if he succeeded, the door was locked.

And if he fell —

Boba swallowed. He thought of his father: No matter how Jango felt, he would always appear brave.

A lot of the time I'm scared, Boba, he had once said. *But if an enemy ever knows you're afraid, you're finished.*

Boba imagined he was as strong and powerful as his father. He imagined himself looking un-afraid — even though that was not how he felt.

He said, "San Hill is raising money for the Sep-aratist cause. The Separatists are united behind Count Dooku —"

The vice-chairs's face twisted angrily. "That's not news! Everyone knows that —"

"I'm not finished," said Boba coolly. "Did you know that a man named Tyranus recruited a bounty hunter named Jango Fett for the Kaminoans to use to create a clone army for the Republic."

"I'd heard things like that," Kos admitted, grow-ing more interested.

"Well, I know this: Dooku and Tyranus are the same person."

The official stared at him in disbelief. After a moment he started to laugh. "You really had me go-ing for a minute," he said. Then his face darkened. "But I have no time to waste — tell me the truth! What do you know?"

Boba hesitated. He knew he was putting his own life in danger by sharing this secret. But it was the only weapon he had.

"He is helping to build two armies," Boba went on slowly. "He has spent millions — billions — on both the droids and the clones. And in the end, only he will benefit from a war."

Boba thought how foolish his own words sounded. But, strangely, the vice-chair seemed to hear them differently.

"Tyranus . . . is Dooku?" he said in a low voice. "But —"

He shook his head. He looked stunned and disbelieving, but Boba could tell that the seeds of doubt had been sown.

"Are you certain of this?" Kos asked after a minute. "This is treason. The highest kind of treason."

Boba nodded. Kos stared, thinking, at the control panel. Finally he said, almost to himself, "I must tell San Hill."

Without another word he steered the airspeeder over to the platform. The craft rocked gently back and forth in the air. The official reached forward and pressed a button. The door onto Level Two slid open.

"Get out," he said curtly. "Before I change my mind and kill you."

Boba jumped out, his heart pounding. It took him a second to get his balance. Then he raced toward the open door.

"Wait —" the vice-chair called from behind him.

Boba turned. The man half-stood in his airspeeder, his blaster drawn.

"You took too long," Kos said in a low voice. "I changed my mind."

CHAPTER TWENTY-ONE

With a gasp Boba turned and sprinted for the door. But before he could reach it, an explosion sounded behind him. He looked back and saw Kos turning to stare at something below his airspeeder. There was the drone of a hoverbike, and another explosive burst that shook the speeder. An instant later, the hoverbike itself came into view. Riding it was a familiar, red-haired figure.

"Aurra," said Boba in disbelief. As he stared she raised her blaster, her blazing eyes fixed on him.

"Got it in one," she said, and fired. There was a second blast as the vice-chair returned her fire, and the hoverbike rocked slightly.

Without hesitation Boba lunged for the airspeeder, diving inside just as the craft shot away from the landing platform. Kos glanced down at him, one hand on the controls, the other on his blaster.

"That's Aurra Sing," the man said grimly. "If she's part of all this . . ."

His voice trailed off. It seemed as though Aurra's sudden appearance made him take Boba even more seriously. The speeder veered and then swooped into a heart-stopping dive. "Take the controls!" Kos shouted as another volley of fire surrounded them.

Boba nodded and jumped into the control seat. The vice-chair turned to monitor Aurra's pursuit. "There are security forces all over Level Two," he said, shaking his head. "There's no way she can get away with this."

"That's not gonna help us if we're dead," retorted Boba. He steered the speeder around a sharp curve in the airshaft, then yanked back on the controls so that the vehicle abruptly shot up, up, into darkness. "I'll see if we can lose her."

Boba stared at the vast space around them, lines of windows and doors reduced to smears of white and green by their speed. Behind them the bike's hum rose to a furious roar. Blasts of white-hot plasma spun past the airspeeder, giving off a scorched smell. As Aurra Sing scored a direct hit, the speeder gave a violent twist to the left. Boba corrected it quickly. He let the speeder go into a dive as Aurra swung in right behind them, then pulled out and soared up again, the bike screaming in pursuit.

"Are we damaged?" Boba yelled above the roar of the engines.

"Not seriously," Kos shouted back. His blaster moved furiously back and forth, trying to get a fix on Aurra Sing, but she was too fast. "I'm going to call for reinforcements —"

Boba swallowed. If the vice-chair called for help, other soldiers would arrive. They'd take Aurra into custody — but they'd take him, too. He'd be questioned about what he had told the official, and —

Boba swallowed. He didn't want to think about what would happen to him if he were brought in for questioning. If what he knew about Dooku and Tyranus became known to San Hill. If it became known to the Count . . .

He couldn't let the lieutenant talk. He hunched over the controls, his hands like ice as they grasped the throttle, then punched commands into the panel.

"There's a price on her head," Boba said. "You'll be well-rewarded by my master for bringing her in. I'll set the comm unit to make a distress call," he lied, pretending to press a small panel of red lights. He glanced back to make sure the vice-chair's eyes were still on the hoverbike whipping through the air behind them. Then he looked up.

Ahead of them, gaps of deeper darkness appeared, more airshafts or maintenance tunnels. Boba kept his sights on one of these, a triangular opening that yawned bigger and bigger as the speeder raced toward it.

"Now!" breathed Boba. He hit the controls, and the speeder swerved suddenly, disappearing into the lightless tunnel.

"What are you doing?" Kos demanded.

"Evasive action," said Boba. Behind them, Aurra's bike swept past the tunnel's entrance. Boba held his breath.

Sure enough, moments later the bike reappeared, barreling up the dark passage after them.

"Get her in your sights now," Boba said, pointing at the figure on the bike, a black shadow against the brilliance of the tunnel's opening. "I'll keep the speeder steady."

Kos fumbled with his blaster. "Hard to see her in this," he muttered. "It's so dark."

"That means it's hard for her to get a fix on you, too," said Boba.

But that was another lie. Aurra Sing had a predator's mind and instincts. She also had a predator's skills. She could see in the dark as keenly as a tuk'ata —

But Kos could not.

Boba held his breath. He slid down as low as he dared, hoping the vice-chair wouldn't notice. But the official was squinting into the darkness, still trying to get his aim fixed on Aurra.

"There she is," he murmured. Boba heard the soft click of the blaster's loading device. Kos raised his arm.

Boba ducked as an explosion ripped through the air beside him.

But it wasn't the official's blast. It was Aurra's.

"Got him!" she crowed triumphantly. Boba grimaced as Kos's tall form toppled over the side of the speeder, to fall soundlessly into the vast and empty shaft. Too late Boba thought of the vice-chair's weapon — it was gone with him into the depths.

And now Boba was alone with Aurra Sing.

"Thought you could betray me? Think again!"

With a dull whine the hoverbike swept toward Boba's airspeeder. He glanced around, hoping to find something he might use as a weapon.

Nothing. He kept his hands on the controls and stared defiantly across the empty darkness at Aurra.

"Everything is for sale on Aargau," she said with a cruel laugh. "I bought myself citizenship. Too bad you won't live long enough to do the same."

Her laughter died, and she stared at Boba with hatred. "No one escapes from me. Boba. I'm the best at what I do."

"My father was better," said Boba in a low, calm voice. His gaze locked with hers as he continued to stare at her, unafraid. As he did, his hand moved slowly, silently, across the control panel. "My father didn't kill for fun. Or out of fear."

"*Fear?*" Aurra's voice rose almost to a scream. Her eyes blazed, and two crimson spots bloomed on her dead-white face. "You think *I'm* afraid? I think it's time I introduce you to the real thing!"

Her face twisted into a mask of rage. She raised her blaster before her face, the bike steady beneath her. "Good-bye, Boba," she said.

Boba ducked. He jammed his hand onto the controls, hitting the REVERSE DIRECTION command. A flaming pulse from Aurra's blaster zoomed a scant meter above his head. At the same moment, the speeder shot backward. He'd hoped it would slam directly into Aurra's bike. Instead it sideswiped it. Aurra shouted furiously as her arms swung and her next blast went wide. Her bike rocked wildly, and she clung to it to keep from plummeting into the abyss.

"Yes!" cried Boba in triumph. The speeder veered back and forth through the passage, barely missing the walls. He finally got control of it, whipping it around so that it soared out from the tunnel and into the vast main shaft. Behind him he could hear Aurra's angry yelling, and the dull thrum of her bike throttling down. He pointed the speeder in the direction he'd come. With a low roar it began to rush back toward the entrance to Level Two.

CHAPTER TWENTY-TWO

Boba knew better than to think he'd lost Aurra for good. She was like a mynock clinging to her prey, difficult to pry loose.

But not impossible. As his speeder drew closer to the entry to Level Two, Boba flicked on the comm unit. Immediately a voice came through the speaker.

"Sir, we've been unable to contact you for some time. Are you all right?"

Boba cleared his throat. "I'm fine," he said, trying to make his voice sound as deep and muffled as possible. "But there's a renegade noncitizen loose on Level Two. She's armed. There may be some casualties —"

And I don't want one of them to be me!

Behind him came the abrupt high drone of Aurra's bike and another explosive burst. The comm unit went dead. Boba leaned over the controls, not taking his eyes from what was ahead of him: the entry to Level Two.

Closer, closer . . . He could see the familiar sign, and the door behind it. Sparks of orange and scarlet flame whistled through the air around him as he drew the speeder alongside the landing platform. Keeping his head low he jumped out, turned, and bolted for the door. He shoved it open, and raced through, onto Level Two.

Immediately the world around him changed color. Instead of darkness, everything shone with a soft green glow. He was in yet another tunnel, but this one was well lit. At one end a sign blinked on and off.

EXIT

Boba whirled. At the other end of the tunnel was another blinking sign.

INTERGALACTICBANK OF KUAT
ENTRANCE ONLY

"That's it!" Boba said aloud. He began to run. From behind the door he'd just left he heard the hoverbike's drone suddenly shut off. He didn't need to look back to know that Aurra Sing was at his heels.

Ahead of him a security droid stood beside the entrance to the bank. "May I see your card, please?" it asked in its mechanized voice.

Boba dug into his pocket. For a second his heart stopped: He'd lost the card!

But no, it was still there. He yanked it out and handed it to the droid. The droid raised the card before its infrared eyes and scanned it. Then it took Boba's hand. There was a flicker of heat as it read his DNA. Then it nodded.

"Very good," it said. "You may enter."

"Stop him!" Aurra's voice raged from the far end of the tunnel.

"You better check her citizen papers," Boba said breathlessly to the security droid. "She's armed and I think her papers are forged."

He pushed open the door and hurried into the bank. Behind him he could hear Aurra's boots racing up to the entrance. Then he heard the droid's calm voice.

"May I see your citizen papers, please?" it asked. The door slammed and locked behind Boba. He grinned as he heard Aurra's voice rise in frustrated rage.

"May I help you?"

It was another droid, this one neatly clad in gold-and-silver hardware. It stood before an immense black wall. Set into the wall were thousands upon thousands of small boxes, each with a number.

"I want to get what is mine," Boba said, gasping. "My father — he left something for me here when he died."

"Of course," said the droid politely. "May I see your card, please?"

Boba handed the card to him. The droid turned and rolled along the front of the wall. Finally it stopped. It punched the card into a slot in the wall. One of the boxes slid open. One of the droid's mechanical arms withdrew something from it. It closed the box, turned, and rolled back to Boba.

"This closes your account," he said, and handed Boba a small leather pouch. The robot stuck the card into another slot inside its chest. There was a hiss and a wisp of smoke. The card had been destroyed.

Boba looked down at the pouch. It seemed awfully small. He opened it, and poured a handful of shining, multicolored credits into his hand.

"Is this all?" he asked. He shook his head. "My father left me a fortune!"

"There was a large withdrawal made from this account today," the droid said in its calm voice.

"Five hundred thousand mesarcs. That is what remains. Your account is now closed," it said with finality, and rolled away.

Boba stared after it in disbelief. Then he looked at the money in his hand. From the passage behind him, he could hear voices.

"Let go of me! I tell you, these papers are legal! I'm allowed to carry a blaster!"

It sounded like Aurra Sing was having a hard time with Aargau security. Even as Boba turned to look, a side door opened. Heavily armed soldiers wearing uniforms identical to the vice-chair's poured into the corridor. He watched as they ran toward where security had detained Aurra Sing, their boots echoing loudly. Moments later he heard Aurra Sing's shout of rage as the soldiers surrounded her.

"No — let me go, you'll never —"

Boba fought back a shiver. He felt no pity for Aurra — she would have killed him as easily as she'd killed the lieutenant, and with more pleasure. But he knew that losing her freedom would be far worse for Aurra Sing than losing her share of his father's fortune.

Still, she probably wouldn't be imprisoned or detained for long. Boba would bet his life on that.

But not right now. Right now, Boba planned to

hang on to every bit of currency he had. He looked at the money in his hand — not a huge fortune, maybe, but still enough to outfit a ship. Still enough to get him off Aargau. He put the money back into the leather pouch and closed it. He put it carefully into his pocket, along with his father's book. Then he turned and began walking quickly down the corridor, back to Level One.

CHAPTER TWENTY-THREE

No one questioned him when he bought the fuel and provisions for his ship. And no one questioned him when he climbed aboard, after obtaining clearance to depart Aargau. Money might not buy happiness, but it bought a lot of other things that were useful.

Boba settled himself in the cockpit of *Slave I*. It felt like coming home again — for the first time. He strapped himself in, hit the controls, and settled back. A moment later he felt the familiar rush and roar of takeoff.

Within moments Aargau was far, far behind him. Boba gazed out the screen at the glittering planet. He wondered briefly about the people he'd seen there. The young clone 9779. The Clawdite Nuri — if that was really his name. The manipulative San Hill.

What would become of them all, Boba wondered? And what would become of the Separatist cause, led by the double-crossing Count Dooku?

And Aurra Sing?

Aurra Sing might be in custody for now, but Boba knew she wouldn't stay there for long. She was too smart for that. And when she got free, she'd come looking for him.

Boba smiled with determination. When he next met up with Aurra Sing, he'd be ready for her. For now, he had other things on his mind.

Boba knew where his immediate future was — with the notorious gangster Jabba the Hutt!

With a grin, he leaned over the control panel and punched in the coordinates for Tatooine.

CLONE WARS
TIMELINE

With the Battle of Geonosis (Episode II), the Republic is plunged into an emerging, galaxy-wide conflict. On one side, the Confederacy of Independent Systems (the Separatists), led by the charismatic Count Dooku and backed by a number of powerful guilds and trade organizations, and their droid armies.

On the other side, the Republic loyalists and their newly created clone army, led by the Jedi. It is a war fought on a thousand fronts, with heroism and sacrifices on both sides. Below is a partial list of some of the important events of the Clone Wars and a guide to where these events are chronicled.

MONTHS (after *Attack of the Clones*)	EVENT
0	**THE BATTLE OF GEONOSIS** *Star Wars*: Episode II *Attack of the Clones* (LFL, May '02)
0	**THE SEARCH FOR COUNT DOOKU** Boba Fett #1: *The Fight to Survive* (SB, April '02)
+1	**THE BATTLE OF RAXUS PRIME** Boba Fett #2: *Crossfire* (SB, November '02)
+1	**THE DARK REAPER PROJECT** The Clone Wars (LEC, May '02)
+1.5	**CONSPIRACY ON AARGAU** Boba Fett #3: *Maze of Deception* (SB, April '03)
+2	**THE BATTLE OF KAMINO** Clone Wars I: *The Defense of Kamino* (DH, June '03)
+3	**THE DEFENSE OF NABOO** Clone Wars II: *Heroes and Scapegoats* (DH, September '03)
+6	**THE HARUUN KAL CRISIS** Mace Windu: *Shatterpoint* (DR, June '03)
+9	**THE DAGU REVOLT** *Escape from Dagu* (DR, March '04)
+12	**THE BIO-DROID THREAT** *The Cestus Deception* (DR, June '04)
+15	**THE BATTLE OF JABIIM** Clone Wars III: *Last Stand on Jabiim* (DH, February '04)

KEY:

DH = *Dark Horse Comics, graphic novels* www.darkhorse.com

DR = *Del Rey, hardcover & paperback books* www.delreydigital.com

LEC = *LucasArts Games, games for XBOX, Game Cube, PS2, & PC platforms* www.lucasarts.com

LFL = *Lucasfilm Ltd., motion pictures* www.starwars.com

SB = *Scholastic Books, juvenile fiction* www.scholastic.com/starwars

BORN TO BE A BOUNTY HUNTER.

When Boba Fett's father, Jango, is killed, Boba must struggle for safety—and vengeance—using his strength, his intelligence, and his father's legacy.

Alone, young Boba Fett must go forth on his path to become a bounty hunter—but first he must escape from the evil Count Dooku.

YOU COULD WIN A
STAR WARS ROOM!

Deadline to enter is
June 30, 2003

For complete details, go to
www.scholastic.com/starwars/

Fill out the form below to be entered for a chance to win a roomful of Star Wars goodies—including video games, books, sheets, blankets, and T-shirts

Scholastic/Star Wars Room Sweepstakes

Name_____

Address_____

City_____ State_____ Zip_____

Male/Female_____ Birth Date_____

Send entry form to: Scholastic/Star Wars Room Sweepstakes, 557 Broadway, 9033, New York, NY 10012-399

www.scholastic.com/starwars

SCHOLASTIC

SWSW403